Dear Reader,

Readers often want to know how I got my start as a writer. When I tell people that my first books were romance novels for Bantam's Loveswept line, they're sometimes surprised. Although this genre may seem completely different from the suspense I write now, the two have more in common than it seems.

For me, every good story has two indispensible components to it: characters to fall in love with and root for, and a mystery to figure out—whether it's an unsolved crime or that confusing and complex emotion that baffles us most of all—love. Even the most detailed murder plot can't compare to the intricate mechanics of the human heart.

In *Heart of Gold,* the first book in a trilogy about a group of college friends, Faith Kinkaid is trying frantically to escape her past, which includes her ex-husband who is on trial for bribery. Despite building a new life for herself and her daughter in the charming seaside town of Anastasia, California, and starting her own bed and breakfast, Faith wants to bring her husband to justice, and agrees to testify against him in a high-profile case. There's just one catch: The Justice Department decides she needs a bodyguard. When Shane Callan shows up on Faith's doorstep, she realizes that her new protector has a deep, vulnerable side beneath his impeccable physique and quick wit. Can Faith overcome her fears to break through Shane's stoic demeanor and give both of them a second chance at love?

Faith and Shane's story touched my heart all those years ago, and I hope that you'll enjoy it as much today.

All my best,

Tami Hoag

Tami Hoag

PRAISE FOR THE BESTSELLERS OF

Tami Hoag

THE ALIBI MAN

"Captivating thriller . . . [Elena] is a heroine readers will want to see more of."

—*Publishers Weekly*

"Hard to put down."

—*The Washington Post*

"A superbly taut thriller. Written in a staccato style that will have readers racing through the pages . . . Will leave readers breathless and satisfied."

—*Booklist*

"A suspenseful tale, with a surprising ending; the author once again has constructed a hard-hitting story with interesting characters and a thrilling plot."

—*Midwest Book Review*

"Elena Estes [is] one of Hoag's most complicated, difficult and intriguing characters. . . . Hoag enhances a tight mystery plot with an over-the-shoulder view of the Palm Beach polo scene, giving her readers an up-close-and-personal look at the rich and famous. . . . *The Alibi Man* is her best work to date."

—BookReporter.com

"An engrossing story and a cast of well-drawn characters."

—Minneapolis *Star Tribune*

"[Hoag] gets better with every book. One of the tautest thrillers I have read for a long while."

—*Bookseller* (U.K.)

"Hoag certainly knows how to build a plot and her skill has deservedly landed her on bestseller lists numerous times."

—*South Florida Sun-Sentinel*

"Hoag has a winner in this novel where she brings back Elena Estes. . . . Hoag is the consummate storyteller and creator of suspense."

—*Mystery News*

"Tami Hoag weaves an intricate tale of murder and deception. . . . A very well-written and thought-out murder/mystery. Hoag is able to keep you guessing and you'll be left breathless until all the threads are unwoven and the killer is revealed."

—FreshFiction.com

PRIOR BAD ACTS

"A snappy, scary thriller."

—*Entertainment Weekly*

"Stunning...Here [Hoag] stands above the competition, creating complex characters who evolve more than those in most thrillers. The breathtaking plot twists are perfectly paced in this compulsive page-turner."

—*Publishers Weekly* (starred review)

"A chilling thriller with a romantic chaser."

—New York *Daily News*

"A first-rate thriller with an ending that will knock your socks off."

—*Booklist*

"An engrossing thriller with plenty of plot twists and a surprise ending."

—*OK!* magazine

"A chilling tale of murder and mayhem."

—*BookPage*

"The in-depth characterization and the unrelenting suspense are what makes *Prior Bad Acts* an outstanding read. Gritty and brutal at times, *Prior Bad Acts* delivers a stunning novel of murder, vengeance and retribution.... Riveting and chilling suspense."

—*Romance Reviews Today*

KILL THE MESSENGER

"Excellent pacing and an energetic plot heighten the suspense.... Enjoyable."

—*Chicago Tribune*

"Everything rings true, from the zippy cop-shop banter, to the rebellious bike messenger subculture, to the ultimate, heady collision of Hollywood money, politics, and power."

—Minneapolis *Star Tribune*

"Hoag's usual crisp, uncluttered storytelling and her ability to make us care about her characters triumph in *Kill the Messenger*."

—*Fort Lauderdale Sun-Sentinel*

"A perfect book. It is well written, and it has everything a reader could hope for.... It cannot be put down.... Please don't miss this one."

—*Kingston Observer*

"[A] brisk read...it demonstrates once again why [Hoag's] so good at what she does."

—*San Francisco Chronicle*

"Action-filled ride...a colorful, fast-paced novel that will keep you guessing."

—*Commercial Appeal*

"High-octane suspense...Nonstop action moves the story forward at a breath-stealing pace, and the tension remains high from beginning to end....Suspense at its very best."

—*Romance Reviews Today*

"Hoag's loyal readers and fans of police procedural suspense novels will definitely love it."

—*Booklist*

"*Kill the Messenger* will add to [Hoag's] list of winners....This is a fast-moving thriller with a great plot and wonderful characters. The identity of the killer is a real surprise."

—*Somerset Daily American*

"Engaging...the triumph of substance over style...character-driven, solidly constructed thriller."

—*Publishers Weekly*

"Hoag upholds her reputation as one of the hottest writers in the suspense genre with this book, which not only has a highly complex mystery, multilayered suspense and serpentine plot, but also great characterizations...an entertaining and expertly crafted novel not to be missed."

—*CurledUp.com*

DARK HORSE

"A thriller as tightly wound as its heroine...Hoag has created a winning central figure in Elena....Bottom line: Great ride."

—*People*

"This is her best to date....[A] tautly told thriller."
—Minneapolis *Star Tribune*

"Hoag proves once again why she is considered a queen of the crime thriller."

—Charleston *Post and Courier*

"A tangled web of deceit and double-dealing makes for a fascinating look into the wealthy world of horses juxtaposed with the realistic introspection of one very troubled ex-cop. A definite winner."

—*Booklist*

"Anyone who reads suspense novels regularly is acquainted with Hoag's work—or certainly should be. She's one of the most consistently superior suspense and romantic suspense writers on today's bestseller lists. A word of warning to readers: don't think you know whodunit 'til the very end."

—*Clute Facts*

BANTAM TITLES BY TAMI HOAG

TAMI HOAG

Heart of Gold

BANTAM BOOKS
NEW YORK

Heart of Gold is a work of fiction. Names, characters, places, and incidents either are the product of the author's imagination or are used fictitiously. Any resemblance to actual persons, living or dead, events, or locales is entirely coincidental.

2010 Bantam Books Mass Market Edition

Published in the United States by Bantam Books, an imprint of The Random House Publishing Group, a division of Random House, Inc., New York.

BANTAM BOOKS and the rooster colophon are registered trademarks of Random House, Inc.

Originally published in paperback in the United States by Bantam Books, a division of Random House, Inc., in 1990.

978-0-553-59335-8

Cover design: Scott Biel
Cover photograph: Comstock Images/Getty Images

Printed in the United States of America

www.bantamdell.com

9 8 7 6 5 4 3 2 1

Heart
of Gold

PROLOGUE

University of Notre Dame, South Bend, Indiana
Spring 1977

"OKAY, EVERYBODY, THIS is it. The final portrait of the Fearsome Foursome. Make sure your caps are on straight, ladies. I'm setting the timer now." Bryan Hennessy hunched over the thirty-five-millimeter camera, fussing with buttons and switches, pausing once to push his glasses up on his straight nose.

Faith Kincaid adjusted the shoulders of her graduation gown and checked her cap, poking back long spirals of burnished gold hair that had escaped the bondage of barrettes. She settled herself and her sunny smile in place.

They stood on the damp grass near the blue expanse of Saint Mary's Lake, not far from the stone grotto that was built into the hillside behind Sacred Heart Church—a replica of the shrine at Lourdes. The clean, cool air was sweet with the scents of spring flowers, new leaves, and freshly cut grass. Bird song mingled with Alice Cooper's *School's Out* blasting from a boom box in a distant dorm.

To Faith's right stood Alaina Montgomery, tall, cool, and poised. To her left stood petite Jayne Jordan, all wide eyes and wild auburn hair. Bryan hustled around to stand behind her, his cap askew. He was tall and athletic with a handsome, honest face and tawny hair that tended to be a bit shaggy, because Bryan tended to forget little details like barber appointments.

These were her three best friends in the entire world. Faith loved them as if they were family. Jayne was artsy and odd, warm and caring. To most people Alaina seemed aloof, but she was fiercely loyal and sharply insightful. Bryan was sweet and eccentric—their surrogate big brother, their confidant.

They had banded together their freshman year.

Four people with nothing in common but a class in medieval sociology. Over the four years that followed they had seen each other through finals and failures, triumphs and tragedies, and doomed romances. They were friends in the truest, deepest sense of the word.

And they were about to graduate and go their separate ways.

Faith sucked in a breath and valiantly blinked back tears.

"Okay, everybody smile," Bryan ordered, his voice a little huskier than usual. "It's going to go off any second now. Any second."

They all grinned engagingly and held their collective breaths.

The camera suddenly tilted downward on its tripod, pointing its lens at one of the white geese that wandered freely around Saint Mary's Lake. The shutter clicked, and the motor advanced the film. The goose honked an outraged protest and waddled away.

"I hope that's not an omen," Jayne said, frowning as she nibbled at her thumbnail.

"It's a loose screw," Bryan announced, digging a

dime out of his pants pocket to repair the tripod with.

"In Jayne or the camera?"

"Very funny, Alaina."

"I think it's a sign that Bryan needs a new tripod," said Faith.

"That's not what Jessica Porter says," Alaina remarked slyly.

The girls giggled as Bryan's blush crept up to the roots of his hair. Faith knew while there had never been any romantic developments within their ranks, outside of his unusual friendship with them Bryan had an active...er...social life.

"If you want a sign, look behind you," he said through gritted teeth as he fussed unnecessarily with the aperture setting on the camera.

Faith turned as her two friends did, and her dark eyes widened at the sight of the rainbow that arched gracefully across the morning sky above the golden dome of the administration building.

"Oh, how beautiful," she said with a gasp, the hopeless romantic in her shining through. Lord, she wasn't even gone yet and already she was feeling nostalgic about the place.

"Symbolic," Jayne whispered.

"It's the diffusion of light through raindrops," Alaina said flatly, crossing her arms in front of her.

Bryan looked up from fiddling with the camera to frown at her, his strong jaw jutting forward aggressively. "Rainbows have lots of magic in them," he said, dead serious. "Ask any leprechaun. It'd do you some good to believe in magic, Alaina."

Alaina's lush mouth turned down at the corners. "Take the picture, Hennessy."

Bryan ignored her, his wise, warm blue eyes taking on a dreamy quality as he gazed up at the soft stripes of color. "We'll each be chasing our own rainbows after today. I wonder where they'll lead us."

They each recited the stock answers they'd been giving faculty, friends, and family for months. Alaina was headed to law school. Jayne was leaving to seek fame and fortune in Hollywood as a writer and director. Bryan had been accepted into the graduate program of parapsychology at Purdue. Faith was headed to a managerial position in a business office in Cincinnati.

"That's where our brains are taking us," Bryan

said, pulling his cap off to comb a hand back through his hair as he always did when he went into one of his "deep-thinking modes." "I wonder where our hearts would take us."

If anyone knew the answer to that, it was Bryan, Faith thought. He was the one they told all their secret dreams to. He was the one she had confided in that she aspired to nothing more than having a husband and children and a small business to run. That was the end of her heart's rainbow.

It probably would have seemed an exceedingly boring dream to Jayne and Alaina. Faith herself admitted it lacked pizzazz and had nothing in the way of driving ambition, but Bryan had assured her it was a wonderful dream.

"That's the question we should all be asking ourselves," Jayne said, wagging a slender finger at her friends. "Are we in pursuit of our true bliss, or are we merely following a course charted by the expectations of others?"

"Do we have to get philosophical?" Alaina asked with a groan, rubbing her temples. "I haven't had my mandatory ten cups of coffee yet this morning."

"Life is philosophy, honey," Jayne explained

patiently, her voice a slow Kentucky drawl that hadn't altered one iota over the four years she'd spent in northern Indiana. The expression on her delicately sculpted features was almost comically earnest. "That's a cosmic reality."

Alaina was nonplussed for a full twenty seconds. Finally she said, "We don't have to worry about you. You'll fit right in in California."

Jayne smiled, her eyes twinkling. "Why thank you."

Faith chuckled at the look on Alaina's face. "Give up, Alaina. You can't win."

Alaina winced and held her hands up as if to ward off the words. "Don't say that. I *abhor* losing."

"Anastasia," Bryan declared loudly. He gave a decisive nod that set the tassel on his cap dancing. The statement would have seemed straight out of left field to anyone who didn't know Bryan Hennessy and the workings of his unconventional mind.

Immediately Faith's heart-shaped face lit up. Anastasia was the small town on California's rugged northern coast where the four of them had spent spring break, a beautiful village nestled in a quiet cove. She smiled now at the memory of the plans they had made to move there and pursue idealistic existences. Jayne's dream had been to have her own farm. Alaina had grudgingly admitted a secret desire to paint. Bryan had wanted to play the role of local mad scientist. An inn with a view of the ocean had been Faith's wish.

"That's right," she said. "We'd all move to Anastasia."

"And live happily ever after." Alaina's tone lacked the sarcasm she had undoubtedly intended. She sounded almost wistful instead.

"Even if we never end up there, it's a nice dream," Jayne said softly.

A nice dream, Faith thought. Something to hang on to, something to take along on the journey into the big world. Like their memories of Notre Dame and each other, warm, golden images they could hold in a secret place in their hearts to be taken out from time to time when they were feeling lonely or blue.

Just the thought made her feel empty inside.

Bryan set the timer on the camera once again, then jogged around to stand behind her. "Who knows? Life is full of crossroads. You can never tell where a path might lead."

And the camera buzzed and clicked, capturing the moment on film for all time. The Fearsome Foursome—wistful smiles canting their mouths, dreams of the future and tears of parting shining in their eyes as a rainbow arched in the sky behind them.

ONE

"MAMA, WHERE DO babies come from?"

Faith stopped in her tracks on her way across the spacious old kitchen. Her gaze shot first to her daughter, Lindy, who sat on the floor pretending to feed her doll from a toy baby's bottle, then lifted skyward. "Couldn't she have waited another year or two?" she whispered urgently.

Lindy looked up at her expectantly, her warm brown eyes shining with love and trust.

Faith tugged a hand through her mop of curls, a gesture of frustration that only added to their disarray. Loose spirals of dark honey-blond shot through with tints of red tumbled across her forehead. She blew at them as she searched frantically for an answer that would satisfy a four-year-old's natural curiosity.

In some distant part of the house a doorbell chimed.

Smiling lovingly at her daughter, Faith breathed a huge sigh of relief. "I have to get the door, sweetie."

Lindy had already lost interest in the conversation. She was all wrapped up in putting her doll to bed in the little toy cradle Mr. Fitz had found for her in one of the attics. Faith started for the front of the house, trying to determine which of the doorbells was ringing.

The house she had purchased to renovate and open as a bed-and-breakfast inn was actually a complex of several houses. The builder, an eccentric sea captain named Argyle Dugan, had added one house onto another over the years as his fortune from his shipping business had increased. The end result after fifty-some years of work was an architectural monstrosity.

The main building was a three-story Victorian mansion, complete with a widow's walk. The front side of the house was graced with a large porch and ornately carved double doors flanked by etched glass panels. These were the doors Faith went toward, following the impatient sound of the bell.

Who could be in such an all-fired hurry, she wondered. It had to be a tourist. No one from Anastasia would be that anxious about anything. She swung back one of the heavy doors, and everything inside her went still.

Elegance was the first word that came to her mind. The man standing on her porch seemed to radiate it. Odd, she thought, because he wasn't dressed in formal attire. He wore black trousers and a dark gray shirt with a black tie. His long gray raincoat hung open, the collar turned up against the brisk wind coming in off the ocean. Still, as he stood there in the late afternoon gloom, with the fog bank for a backdrop, there was a sense of elegance about him. Elegance and danger.

Faith's gaze darted nervously to the suitcase on the floor of the porch, then back up a good six feet to the man's face. He was handsome. No one could have argued that fact. His was a lean, angular face with high cheekbones, a bold straight nose, and pale gray eyes that stared down at her with wary disdain. There was something of the arrogant aristocrat in his looks, and something that wasn't quite civilized in his cool silver eyes. The wind ruffled his night black hair, which was cut short on the sides—for practicality rather than fashion, she guessed.

He looked like a no-nonsense sort. A no-nonsense sort with no sense of humor.

"I'm sorry," Faith said at last, a thin nervous tremor in her voice. The fingers of her right hand automatically went to the necklace at her throat, sliding the heart medallion back and forth. "We won't be open for business for a few more days. I can give you directions to—"

"Are you Faith Gerrard?" His low voice made her think of whiskey and smoke and rumpled sheets.

"Kincaid," she corrected him, swallowing hard. Heaven help her, the man had a bedroom voice. Tingles raced over her skin like hedonistic fingers. She felt as if his voice had reached out and touched her intimately. Knock it off, Faith, she told herself, this is no time to fall into a romantic fantasy. "Umm— Faith Kincaid. Yes, I am."

He reached into an inside pocket of his overcoat and extracted what looked to Faith like a wallet, but when he flipped it open, there was a gold shield inside, as well as an identification card. His photograph frowned out at her with the kind of brooding quality that made GQ models rich.

"Shane Callan. The Justice Department sent me."

"Ah." Faith nodded, one hand gripping the door for support as her knees quivered. In spite of his heart-stopping looks, she should have recognized the glower. The people she had encountered in her dealings with the Justice Department had all been similarly humorless. With good reason, she supposed. Well, Mr. Callan's humor wasn't likely to improve when he heard what she had to say.

Outwardly she appeared calm and collected. She even managed a perfectly pleasant smile. She had learned that kind of control as a tool of self-preservation during her marriage to Senator William Gerrard. In truth her heart was racing and her hands were clammy. Just do it, Faith, she told herself as nerves scrambled around inside her stomach like crabs on the beach.

"I told Mr. Banks it wasn't necessary to send you." The words came tumbling out of her mouth, defying punctuation. "I'm sorry you came all this way for nothing, Mr. Callan. You'll find a hotel in Anastasia. Good day."

Shane stared in disbelief at the door that had just

been shut in his face. This wasn't quite the greeting he had imagined receiving from Senator Gerrard's ex-wife. But then, he admitted, he hadn't imagined the senator's ex-wife would be running around in a worn-out Notre Dame sweatshirt and faded old jeans that lovingly molded her curvy little figure either.

He could easily call to mind every detail of the photographs he had casually glanced at when going through her file. Silk and mink. Hundred-dollar hairstyles and flawless makeup. The woman who had answered the door had looked more like a maid than the owner of the Keepsake Inn.

Pretty, he noted, then stubbornly ignored the sweet ache of physical attraction. It didn't make a bit of difference to him that she had the kind of feminine appeal that made the average man's blood heat to the boiling point. His blood was only just simmering, and he was in complete control of it.

Faith Gerrard, or Kincaid, or whatever the hell she wanted to call herself, was no woman to get tangled up with. Senator Gerrard had found her angelic expression and sparkling dark eyes irresistible too. Now the senator was under indictment for bribery, racketeering, and conspiracy to defraud the federal government, and Faith was lolling her days away under protection of the Justice Department—probably because she had cut some kind of deal for herself.

He punched the doorbell again, irritation rubbing against his raw nerve endings. He didn't need this. He didn't need this wimpy assignment, didn't need the headache a woman like Faith was bound to inspire. But orders—no matter how distasteful—were orders. Banks had sent him there to do a job. No delectable little slip of a woman was going to keep him from doing it.

When she swung the door back on its hinges this time, Shane snatched up his bag and stepped inside in a move more graceful than any door-to-door salesman had ever mastered.

"Oh dear," Faith murmured, wide-eyed. Agent Callan looked awfully determined to stay. The prospect sent another flurry of tingles down her limbs. "Umm—Mr. Callan, I don't think you understand. It's like I told you—"

"I know what you told me," Shane said, staring down at her. Annoyance scratched at his temper when he realized his gaze was being drawn to the O of Notre Dame on her sweatshirt, where the letter distinctly outlined her nipple.

He cleared his throat and glared at her as if her body's involuntary response had been planned deliberately to distract him. "Now let me tell you a thing or two, Mrs. Gerrard. Mr. Banks believes you need protection. I take orders from Mr. Banks. When the Justice Department sends an agent to look after you, you can't just say no thank you and slam the door in his face. That may work with encyclopedia salesmen, but it doesn't work with me."

Faith stared open-mouthed at him for a full thirty seconds before she could scrape together a response. With her small chin set at a mutinous angle, she decided to fight arrogance with arrogance—provided she could fake it. Arrogance wasn't high on the list of things this man was making her feel.

"The last I knew the United States was a democracy, not a police state," she said in her most businesslike tone. "My taxes pay your wages, Mr. Callan. That makes me your boss."

Immediately her imagination raced to consider the possibilities of having this government hunk at her beck and call. Her skin heated.

"That's an interesting theory," Shane said, successfully suppressing a chuckle. She was a feisty little thing...but that didn't interest him in the least.

In an effort to keep his eyes off her breasts, his gaze wandered lazily around the spacious entrance hall, taking in the heavy mahogany reception desk, the polished walnut wainscoting, and the freshly papered wall above it. "Maybe you should join a debate club."

Faith cast a longing glance at his shins, wondering what the penalty would be for giving a federal agent a good swift kick. Her thoughts segued quickly into speculation about what his legs looked like under his fashionable trousers. Probably muscular, probably hairy, prob—

With a little gasp of surprise at the suddenly sensuous bend her mind was taking, she snapped her gaze back to focus just to the right of his handsome face.

"I really don't appreciate your attitude, Mr. Callan," she said primly. "You're awfully snippy."

Snippy? Shane had to rub a hand across his mouth to hide his amusement. He'd been called a lot of things in his day. Snippy was not among them. Damn, she was cute... but it wasn't his job to think so.

When his gaze swung back to her, it held the sharp glint of steel. "Mrs. Gerrard, the federal government is willing to spend time and manpower protecting that pretty little fanny of yours. The least you could do is cooperate."

"All I've done from the start of this nightmare is cooperate," Faith insisted, trying unsuccessfully to ignore the fact that he'd commented on her derriere. She crossed her arms in front of her to keep from running her hands over the seat of her jeans. "I've been a veritable paragon of cooperation."

"Mama?"

Shane watched with keen interest as Faith went to her daughter and knelt down. The little girl was adorable. Four years old, the file had said, a cherub with a heart-shaped face framed by red-gold waves. There was a smudge of flour on her button nose. Her eyes were the same sable shade as her mother's, and they sparkled with curiosity as she peered over Faith's shoulder at him.

"Who's that, Mama?" she asked shyly.

"Nobody, sweetheart," Faith said, trying nonchalantly to scoot around so Agent Callan wouldn't be able to stare at her behind.

Shane scowled. Nobody, huh? The little one smiled sweetly and waved a chubby hand at him. Something caught hard in his chest. He tried to ignore the feeling as he awkwardly lifted a hand to return her salute and then self-consciously ran it back through his hair.

Rolling her eyes, Faith frowned at him, then turned back to Lindy. "Sweetie, it's almost time for supper. Why don't you take your baby to your room and put her to bed?"

Lindy shook her head, an impish smile curving her mouth. "She's not sleepy."

"She will be by the time you get to your room," Faith assured her. She pressed a kiss to her daughter's forehead. "Go on now. Be a good girl."

Tossing Shane a heart-stealing smile, Lindy snuggled her doll, then turned and headed back down the hall. Faith remained on her knees for a moment, watching her daughter walk away. A day didn't go by that she didn't thank God for Lindy. When everything else in her world had seemed bleak and hopeless, Lindy had unfailingly provided her with sweetness and light. She was doing it still, Faith realized as she rose and turned to face Shane Callan once more.

"I imagine we can clear all this up with a phone call," she said pleasantly. After all, she'd been raised to have good manners. And she had learned to deal with all sorts of people during her twelve years in Washington.

Of course, none of them had rattled her the way this man had. Not even the Arab sheik who had offered her former husband nine camels for her.

She could feel Callan's gaze as he followed her. Electricity ran down her back in warm rivulets. Beneath her sweatshirt her nipples were tight knots. She became suddenly, acutely aware of her rear end. He must have been staring at it, the infuriating man. She tugged her sweatshirt down and tried not to wiggle as she led the way down the hall.

The inn's office was a small room, neatly kept, but crowded with a walnut desk and a four-drawer filing cabinet. The wallpaper was feminine and flowery with a background that women probably called mauve, Shane thought.

He shook his pounding head in disgust. Lord, he was losing his edge, going on about wallpaper. But then he had known he was losing his edge. He had just spent a week in a hospital nursing a bullet wound that proved it. Now Banks had stuck him on this glorified guard duty. After three years spent in undercover work, this was probably just the kind of assignment he needed, but that didn't make him like it any better.

He leaned against the doorjamb in a negligent pose as Faith went behind the desk. All he wanted right now was a hot meal and a soft pillow. The thought of a hot, soft woman was judiciously edited from the list as he dragged his gaze from Faith for the hundredth time. He was nursing a major case of jet lag and the remnants of a hangover. For two cents he would have bid this assignment adieu and gone south for some sun, but it was too late for that.

To escape his own introspection, Shane forced himself to study Faith with the cool, impersonal professionalism he was known for. A frown tugged at her mouth, but it wasn't petulance. She looked upset as she sat in the old swivel chair behind the desk and dialed the phone number from memory. While she waited for someone to pick up on the other end of the line, she studiously avoided looking at him. The fingers of her right hand toyed nervously with the small pendant that hung on a chain around her neck.

Nice neck, he thought, his mind drifting traitorously. It was a sleek ivory column that was mostly exposed because her dark blond hair had been cut into a mop of unruly curls. The smooth, soft-looking skin beckoned for the touch of a man's lips. Unconsciously he ran his tongue over his, then ground his teeth at the surge of desire that stirred in his loins.

"Mr. Banks, please," Faith said to the receptionist on the other end of the line.

Her eyes darted to the man filling her office doorway. When she met his cool appraisal, her gaze dived to the ink blotter. Lord above, the man was a hunk!

She scolded herself for thinking about that. What did it matter to her that Shane Callan's looks could have put any Hollywood star to shame? It didn't. What did it matter to her that this gorgeous tower of masculinity found her fanny fascinating? It didn't matter a bit. She reminded herself he was thoroughly irritating, and as soon as she spoke with Mr. Banks, he was going to be gone.

"I'd like a tour of the house right away," Shane said, a smug smile tilting the corners of his lips.

Faith sat back in her desk chair and gave him the most disgruntled look she could muster, considering she found his smile utterly sexy. She didn't need sexy. She didn't need Adonis lurking around her house, making her bones go limp every time she looked at him. How would she ever get any work done going around with limp bones?

But John Banks had just shown her that he was not only as emotionless as the Rock of Gibraltar, he was as immovable as well. He had told her in no uncertain terms that she was stuck with Agent Handsome, whether she thought she needed him or not.

"I don't understand your attitude, Mrs. Gerrard," Shane said, perching a hip on one corner of her desk. He folded his arms across his chest. "You're being offered protection. All things considered, you ought to be grateful."

"It's not that I don't appreciate the thought," Faith said sincerely, her sable eyes begging for understanding. Her slim shoulders lifted in a shrug. "It's just that I don't need protection. You'll be wasting your time." And upsetting my hormones, she added silently.

"That's not what Banks thinks. Your ex-husband and his pals have been making noises about you testifying in the DataTech trial next month."

"I know William." She winced a bit at the memory of the man she had once pledged to love until death. "He's very good at threats, but I don't think he has the guts to make good on this one."

Doubt immediately surfaced inside her. She didn't believe William would physically hurt her, but then she'd been wrong about William Gerrard time and again. There was a time when she hadn't believed him capable of betraying his country either.

"It doesn't take much in the way of guts to hire someone else to carry out threats," Shane said softly, almost gently.

Faith refused to consider that possibility. It was too remote, too unreal, like something from a television crime drama. To reassure herself, she said, "He doesn't have any idea where I am."

Shane simply lifted an eyebrow as if to say that was a minor problem that could be easily solved.

Rubbing a trembling hand across her forehead, Faith heaved a ragged sigh. She didn't want to deal with any of this. She and her daughter were building a new life there on the northern coast of California. She didn't want William Gerrard to intrude in any way.

More than anything, she wanted to forget about

the way he had lied to her, the way he had used her and Lindy. She didn't want any memories of that tainting her new life. Shane Callan was a reminder that she didn't have any say in the matter—at least not until the trial was over.

"That tour, Mrs. Gerrard?"

"Please don't call me that," she whispered. "I divorced William Gerrard ten months ago."

"Just in the nick of time," Shane muttered half under his breath as he rose and motioned for her to precede him out the door. It wouldn't do for him to forget that she may well have played a role in her ex-husband's scheme. He reminded himself of that and pushed away the foreign feelings of sympathy that had been niggling at him as he'd stared down into Faith's fathomless brown eyes.

Faith just caught his comment and bit back a retort. What did she care what Callan thought of her? Why waste her breath telling Shane Callan that a charming politician on his way to big things had swept a naive girl from the farm country of Ohio off her feet, that he had wooed her with words of love because he had believed she would be an asset to his "down-home" image. What would a man like Shane Callan know of the heartbreak she had lived with bound to a man who didn't love her by vows she felt she couldn't break?

No, she told herself. She was stuck with Shane Callan. The best thing she could do would be to ignore him.

Pulling herself up to her full height, she tilted her head back and looked Callan in the eye. Heavens, he was tall—six feet four if he was an inch—and his shoulders seemed to take up half the room. There was an awful lot of him to ignore, and every inch was to-die-for handsome.

"I'll show you around the house and give you a room, but I'll ask that you stay out of the way," she said primly. "This inn opens in five days, and there's still a great deal of work to be done. I don't need some brooding cop hanging around leaving the toilet seats up."

Shane forgot himself and let go a rusty-sounding laugh. Damn, she had more spunk than he would ever have given her credit for. He had to force a frown; he wasn't supposed to find her amusing... or cute...or alluring...

"Take your time doing the work," he said as he followed her down the hall toward the central staircase. "You won't be opening for business until after the trial."

Faith wheeled on him with a stern look that brought him up short. "I most certainly will. I have guests booked. My friends have been staying here helping me get ready for the grand opening."

"Friends?"

Shane stopped her on the stairs with a hand on her upper arm. Turning her around, his fingertips brushed the soft outer swell of her breast. The shock of the contact instantly derailed his train of thought. How would it feel to cup his hand beneath that firm, womanly globe of flesh? Heat surged through him in a wildfire of desire.

Locking his gaze on hers, he held his breath tightly in his lungs and willed his concentration back. The strain came through his sandpaper voice. "Nobody said anything to me about your having friends."

"I don't doubt the concept is foreign to you," Faith said weakly, her breath running out of her in fluttering ribbons.

Her breast seemed to heat and swell at his touch. A burning sensation ran from her chest downward to pool and swirl in the most feminine part of her.

Self-preservation made her jerk her arm from Shane's grasp.

"Jayne and Alaina are out running errands for me right now," she said, trying to turn her mind away from sex. To her dismay she found her mental power steering had gone out, and her thoughts kept veering back to the feel of Callan's hand on her breast. It had been forever since a man had touched her, even accidentally. Stifling a groan, she cleared her throat and forced her thoughts back to the conversation. "I'm lucky to have such good friends. Setting up an inn takes a lot of work."

And a lot of money, Shane figured, dragging his gaze off the well-rounded female fanny that was now at eye level three steps ahead of him. The cost of this property alone, which was in a prime location along the coast less than two hours north of San Francisco, had to be astronomical.

"A thrifty way to invest your divorce settlement," he commented mildly as he joined her in the second-floor hall.

Faith's dark eyes flashed. "The money I took from William in the divorce was for Lindy. All I wanted for myself was to get out."

"Ah, well, what would you need with alimony

when you no doubt had your cut of the money from the defense contracts safely stashed away," he said, pushing his coat back and tucking his hands into his trouser pockets.

Faith sucked in her breath. She knew William had tried to implicate her in his scheme after the fact. She also knew that the Justice Department had found nothing to substantiate his claims. That Shane Callan nevertheless believed she was guilty hurt her pride. She might have told herself it didn't matter what he thought, but that didn't take the sting out of his snide remarks.

"I bought this inn with a bank loan and money invested by friends. That's the truth. Believe it or don't." With that she turned on the heel of her sneaker and marched down the hall like a petite field general.

As she took Callan through the various floors and wings of the rambling house, she recited the history of the place in the manner of an uninspired tour guide. She hoped she was boring him to death. He was nothing but trouble, and she didn't want him anywhere near her, she reminded herself, resolutely pushing the memory of the sensation of his fingers on her breast far, far away.

Setting a brisk pace, she led him down one hall after another. They passed through guest rooms and sitting rooms. On the main floor they wandered through a library and a room Lindy called the "Aminal Room," where Captain Dugan had covered the walls with mounted heads of exotic beasts. They cut through the ballroom, where murals adorned three walls and a grand piano sat near an outer wall that was made almost entirely of glass.

Agent Callan didn't seem to appreciate the high ceilings and polished wood floors or the antiques or the views of the ocean. As Faith took him from the Victorian section of the house to the smaller Italianate section, then back to the Cape Cod and the original two-room cottage, his mood grew darker than the beard that shadowed his lean cheeks. By the time they arrived back at their starting point, he was swearing under his breath.

"This damn place is indefensible," he said, scowling at Faith as if it were her fault. "There are so many ways in and out of here, it would take an army to watch them all."

Faith laughed. This situation was so weird it was funny. What did the man think, that she should live in a bomb shelter?

"Apparently Captain Dugan never considered the paranoid needs of the average G-man when he built the place," she said dryly, then checked her watch and sighed. "If you'll excuse me, Mr. Callan, I have to see to dinner."

His scowl bounced right off her as she turned with her pretty nose in the air and headed for the kitchen. With grudging admiration Shane gave her points for standing up to him. She had a lot of sass . . . and a fabulous fanny.

"Ms. Kincaid?" His low, rough voice made her turn around in her tracks. "I need a room."

Faith nibbled at her lip. Her first impulse was to stick him in the farthest corner of the house, but she doubted he would go for that.

"Which room is yours?"

Before she could catch herself, she looked right at the door to her bedroom, not three feet from Callan. Shane gave her a sly, sexy smile and checked the room behind him, the room directly across the hall from hers.

"I'll take this one." Before she could voice a protest, he picked up his suitcase and went inside.

The room was small but tastefully decorated with period antiques. A fancy reproduction of a hurricane lamp squatted on a square oak table that served as a nightstand. There was an afghan folded on the seat of a pressed-back rocker in one corner. A pitcher and bowl sat on an embroidered runner on top of the dresser. The decor was decidedly feminine. Tiny flowers and vines covered the cream-colored background of the wallpaper. Ruffles and flounces adorned the four-poster bed. Dried wreaths hung on the wall, and the scent of something sweet drifted on the air. There was a very homey feel to the place.

Shane frowned. Home. What would he know about it? It had been so long since he'd been home, the memory of it seemed unreal to him.

Going through a routine that was automatic, he popped open his suitcase and began to unpack. The first thing that came out was a book of poetry. The second was a sterling flask of Irish whiskey. He poured himself a shot and tossed back half of it. He needed it. His head was pounding, his shoulder hurt like the very devil, and a black mood was crawling around the edges of his consciousness.

Recruits were taught that agents didn't drink on the job. Shane had been on the job long enough to know agents did whatever they had to do.

He unpacked his clothes and hung them neatly in

the small armoire that stood along one wall. He hung up his raincoat as well, then carefully shrugged off his shoulder harness and placed his gun on the dresser.

Pain burned in his left shoulder as he gingerly rotated his arm and felt threads of scar tissue tear loose inside where the bullet wound was still healing. Kicking off his shoes, he bent and removed the .25 caliber pistol strapped to his ankle.

Finally he stretched out on the bed to allow himself a few moments' relaxation. That elusive sweet scent—powder-soft, flower-delicate—drifted up from the pillow as he eased his head down. The image of Faith Kincaid filled his head.

She had surprised him, and dammit, he hated surprises. He had expected her to welcome the protection the government was offering her as a key witness in what the press called DataScam. Instead she had politely said no thank you and closed the door on him as if he were a Boy Scout selling magazine subscriptions. He had expected her to be decked out in designer finery, trailing a plume of expensive fragrance. Instead she looked like an ordinary housewife who'd been caught with no makeup on.

The lack of lipstick and eye shadow didn't make her any less appealing. Lighting a cigarette, Shane ground his teeth at the memory of the way her backside filled out a pair of jeans. His fingertips had discovered some equally delectable curves hidden under her sweatshirt. He nearly groaned aloud at the memory of her soft, womanly fullness.

No doubt about it, Faith Kincaid was a lovely little package. Too bad there was a very good chance she was a scheming little backstabber as well.

"Arrogant jerk!"

Faith's knife sliced down, viciously mutilating the head of lettuce on the chopping block. She needed to take her temper out on something. Better it be the salad she had to prepare for dinner than Agent Callan's thick head. And it seemed infinitely safer to recall her anger with him than to recall such things as his rare sexy smile and the seductive undercurrent of attraction that ran between them like a billion watts of electricity. Under her breath she muttered a stream of uncomplimentary observations about the man as she threw the lettuce into a bowl. Errant shreds of roughage flew all over the blue-tiled counter.

Nothing, *nothing* galled her more than being accused of something she hadn't done. She was a decent, honorable person, a woman of integrity. When she had discovered William Gerrard was involved in a scam to profit from defense contracts, she had gone straight to the authorities and told them all she knew. She had done the patriotic thing, and now she was paying for it by having to put up with a cynical cop who seemed to think she had masterminded the entire evil plan.

While she hacked up a stalk of celery, she tried her best to dismiss the incident on the staircase. Unfortunately the memory of that incidental contact was a stubborn one. She thought she could still feel the tips of his fingers pressing into her breast. A traitorous flush washed over her, and Faith cursed herself and her breast and Shane Callan and all men everywhere.

With brown eyes narrowed and sparking with anger, she planted a huge onion on the chopping block and bisected it with one violent slice of the knife. Little flecks of white exploded off the wooden surface as she chopped with a vengeance.

"Mama, can I help?" Lindy asked, tugging at Faith's pant leg.

"No, Lindy, this is Mama's work," she said, dismissing her daughter and letting her mind turn back to nasty speculation as to the species occupying space in Shane Callan's family tree.

"But I'm a mama too," Lindy protested crossly. "I put my baby to bed, and now I have to make supper."

"Not tonight."

Lindy stamped her foot in a rare show of temper. "Yes!"

"Lindy." Faith heaved an impatient sigh, put her knife down, and lifted a hand to push her bangs back from her forehead. Burning, stinging tears rose immediately in her eyes from the strong onion scent that drenched her fingers.

Biting her tongue on a string of curses, she grabbed a towel and sank to the floor with her back to the cabinets, feeling frustrated and defeated and tired and just plain mad. Lindy stared at her with wide, worried brown eyes.

"Don't cry," she said, her bottom lip trembling threateningly. "I don't like it when you cry, Mama."

Faith held her arms out to her little daughter and was immediately engulfed in a warm hug, the smell of baby powder and little girl washing over her. "I'm sorry, sweetie. Mama's not having a very good day."

Lindy hugged her tighter and patted her back consolingly. "Poor Mama."

Poor Mama, Faith agreed silently, as she took comfort from holding her child. She had foolishly believed all her troubles had been left behind. The width of a continent separated her from the man who had imprisoned her in an empty, miserable life. But her problems weren't over. There was one big, disgustingly handsome one right down the hall, waiting for her to call him to dinner.

"A mansion in the mist," the man said softly to himself as he lowered his binoculars and sat back against the plush leather seat of the rented Jag. An evil smile turned his lips upward as he ran a loving hand over the gun that lay on top of a folder full of illegally reproduced Justice Department reports. Briefly he wondered how long it would be before anyone noticed that one lowly secretary had never returned from her hastily requested vacation. Just as quickly the thought was dismissed, and he stared once again at the inn perched at the cliff's edge. "A mansion in the mist. How very Gothic. How very apropos. The perfect setting for a murder."

TWO

"Is that *really* necessary, Mr. Callan?" Faith asked as she passed him the salad bowl.

Shane followed the path of her startled dark eyes to the place where his tweed jacket opened just enough to give her a glimpse of the nine-millimeter Smith and Wesson strapped to his shoulder.

"It's just part of the uniform," he said blandly, his cool, level gaze drinking in her appearance. She had traded her sweatshirt for a soft, aquamarine V-neck sweater, but she still wore no makeup and no jewelry except for the simple heart necklace.

Even so, he had all he could do to pull his gaze off her.

"It's a fashion accessory I'd rather not see around my home," Faith said weakly. Strange, contradictory thrills ran through her at the thought that Shane Callan would look good holding a gun.

Shane gave her a dangerous smile full of predatory promise. "Then stop staring at my chest. Please pass the pepper."

Trying to ignore the rough sensuality of his low voice, Faith handed him the pepper mill. His hand closed around it, briefly trapping her fingers beneath his. Like metal filings to magnets, her gaze flew up to meet his as her heart vaulted into her throat. Shane's expression gave away nothing, yet the message that passed between them was very clear on a basic, instinctive level. Faith shivered as he allowed her to draw her hand away.

Holy smoke, she thought, staring down at her plate. In twelve years of marriage she had never experienced such a powerful physical reaction as she had when this man touched her—and he didn't even do it on purpose. What rotten luck that she would find that kind of attraction with a man who was a total creep. A handsome creep, but a creep just the same, she decided, trying to dredge up some of the anger she had wallowed in earlier.

Shane took note of the color that tinted Faith's fair complexion, then forced his attention away again as he felt his body responding to subliminal messages. Dammit, she got him hot—and she wasn't even trying! Lord help him if she ever decided it would be to her advantage to seduce him, Shane thought, disgusted with this unusual lack of self-control.

They were seated at one of several tables that occupied the inn's large, elegant dining room. Apparently Captain Dugan had built this section of the house during the boom years of his shipping trade, he thought, as he took in the white marble fireplace and the heavy mahogany antiques that filled the room.

Surreptitiously he studied the other members of the dinner party. Across from him sat Jayne Jordan, petite and pretty with rather funky taste in clothes. She wore a man's houndstooth jacket over a silk-and-lace camisole. Opposite Faith sat her other friend, Alaina Montgomery, all cool poise and designer labels.

The women made an interesting trio, Shane mused

as he absently raised a forkful of salad to his mouth and began to chew. His eyes widened as his teeth stopped working in midchew. He glanced at the other two women seated at the table. They both wore similar looks and had frozen with their forks lifted halfway to their mouths.

At the other end of the table Alaina Montgomery swallowed first and delicately dabbed at her lush mouth with a rose-colored cloth napkin. "Onion salad," she said with a hint of humor in her husky alto voice. "Is this a new recipe, Faith?"

Faith took in the expressions of the other adults at the table. What had she done to the salad? As everyone watched her expectantly, she took a bite of hers and choked.

Lord, she'd thrown the entire chopped onion into the bowl!

"Sorry," she said, shooting Shane a look that mixed amusement with annoyance. "I guess I was a little distracted in the kitchen tonight."

"Any other surprises we ought to know about?" he asked, one dark brow crooking upward as he took the bread basket she thrust at him.

"I laced your coffee with arsenic," she said sweetly.

He barely managed to keep his laughter locked in his chest. His eyes sparkled with rare good humor. "How thoughtful of you."

"What's arsnip, Mama?" Lindy asked, pausing in her game of stir-the-peas-on-the-plate.

"That's something we give to very special guests, like Mr. Callan," Faith said, her expression deadpan.

Something about him just brought out the devil in her, she thought, as she leaned over to cut her daughter's meat. She had never teased William that way. Of course, expending emotion on William Gerrard had been a wasted effort. She had learned that early on in their marriage.

What William had wanted from her had nothing to do with emotion. That had been a very unpleasant reality for a young woman who had a wealth of love inside her. For a long time she had waited and hoped and prayed he would change, that she could change him, but over and over her love had been tossed back in her face. Her husband hadn't had the time or the capacity to love another human being. His hunger for power and money had overridden that.

"Gee, Mom, I think I'm grown-up enough to cut my own meat," Shane said dryly.

Faith jerked her head up, her startled gaze colliding with his. Out of habit she had sliced Lindy's roast, then her own, and had somehow ended up with her knife on Shane's plate. Her breath stuck in her throat as she stared at him. Lord, he was good-looking, and he was definitely grown-up enough to cut his own meat.

Managing to scrape together some bravado, she sat back and gave him a sassy look. "Well, you didn't tell me you were housebroken."

"Heck, yes, ma'am." He sent her a dazzling smile. "I'm potty trained and everything."

"What a pleasant surprise," Faith commented, fighting to keep a straight face. She refused to be charmed by a man who thought she was a criminal.

"Don't take it personally, Mr. Callan," Jayne Jordan said, her eyes sparkling with laughter as she looked across the table at him. She tossed her mane of auburn hair over her shoulder as she shot a teasing grin at her friend. "Faith is hypermaternal. She'll probably try to button your coat up for you too."

Shane couldn't stop the fleeting image of Faith

*un*buttoning his clothes. Stabbing a chunk of beef, he cursed his suddenly rebellious libido.

"I'll try to stop myself short of spitting on my fingers and combing your hair," Faith pledged.

"Gee, thanks."

As everyone settled into the task of devouring the excellent meal, Shane focused his attention on work. This case was a far cry from what he was accustomed to, but he was determined to do the job right. He had already been on the phone chewing out Banks about the shoddy background work that had been done. If he had been a few days later in getting here, the place would have been crawling with suspects. Faith Kincaid and her DataScam testimony might have been lying at the bottom of a cliff, shoved off by a supposed guest of the Keepsake Inn.

"What will you tell your guests when you call to cancel their reservations?"

"Nothing," Faith said with false calm as she buttered a dinner roll. "I'm not going to call them, because I'm not going to cancel."

"Yes, you are," Shane said, carefully enunciating each word for emphasis. He leaned toward her, trying to intimidate her with his size as well as his cool stare.

"No, I'm not," Faith said just as clearly. She leaned forward as well, a dizzying rush of adrenaline surging through her as she met his challenge. It was a heady feeling, one that walked a fine line between anger and passion. As she looked up at him, she felt herself teetering on that line.

"Faith," Alaina said cautiously, "if Mr. Callan thinks—"

"If Mr. Callan thinks, I'll consider it a real bonus for my tax dollar." She could see a muscle jerk in his strong jaw, but the warning didn't stop the recklessness he inspired in her. "Canceling my grand opening isn't any more necessary than Mr. Callan's presence here is."

Tension sang in the air like an overloaded power line as brown eyes warred with gray. Faith thought she could feel the heat of his rising temper rolling off him like steam.

Lindy, happily oblivious to what was going on between the adults at the table, picked up the oddly shaped bun on her plate and held it out toward Shane. "Lookit," she said, giving him her shy smile. "I made it all by myself."

The anger drained out of Shane as Faith Kincaid's little daughter caught his attention. What a heart stealer. So sweet, so innocent. When was the last time anything that pure and good had come within ten feet of him, he wondered.

Giving the bun a serious look, he cleared his throat and said, "That's very nice."

Lindy beamed. "It's a bun."

Faith released a pent-up breath and ran a slightly unsteady hand over her daughter's hair. Lindy to the rescue again, she thought with a tender smile. No telling where her reckless abandon would have landed her had she pushed Callan another step. He was obviously a man whose authority was seldom questioned. "Lindy likes to help me in the kitchen. Don't you, sweetie?"

"Uh-huh." To Shane she explained, "I'm gonna be a mama when I grow up." She slid down off her chair and went around the table to present her doll to Shane. "This is my baby. Her name is Mary."

Ordinarily Faith would have herded her daughter back to her chair with a gentle reprimand for disturbing a guest's dinner, but she was too busy watching Callan handle the situation. Something in his expression changed drastically as he looked at Lindy. The icy quality melted from his gray eyes, all the hard edges of his face softened. He looked almost... vulnerable. He accepted Lindy's doll a bit awkwardly, but with all the care he would have shown had Mary been a real baby rather than a hand-me-down doll with frizzy brown hair and one eye that liked to stick shut.

It hit Faith that she knew nothing about him. Perhaps he had a wife and children of his own someplace, and he was separated from them because he had to be here watching out for her. Maybe he was lonely. Maybe... maybe she was romanticizing the situation, as usual.

Oh, Faith, she sighed inwardly, haven't you learned your lesson? There's no such thing as happily ever after. You, of all people, should know that.

"See," Lindy said to Shane, pointing at her doll. "She has real eyelashes."

Shane bent his dark head down as he handed the doll back to the little girl. "She's a very pretty baby," he said gravely.

Lindy readily agreed. "Uh-huh. She used to be my mama's baby when Mama was little like me." She cradled the doll expertly in her arms and looked up at Shane. "Do you know where babies come from?"

All three women at the table stifled giggles as the super-cool Agent Callan blushed like a teenager. Even his ears turned red.

"Uh—umm—well," Shane stammered.

Lindy gazed up at him, patiently waiting for an answer. He looked to Faith, his expression comically desperate. She offered nothing more helpful than a placid smile.

Jayne finally took pity on him and came around the table to take Lindy's hand. "Let's go get that pudding we made this afternoon, sugar plum."

Her earthshaking question easily dismissed, Lindy gave Shane a look that was pure flirtation and said, "It's chocolate."

"Do you have children, Mr. Callan?" Faith asked nonchalantly, not willing to admit to herself that she was holding her breath in anticipation of his answer.

"No." Shane stared at his plate, angry at feeling so unsettled. Dammit, Faith Kincaid had thrown him badly enough, he didn't need her daughter knocking his feet out from under him as well. It was just that they seemed so . . . *normal.* And everything he had seen in the last few years had been a perversion of normal life.

"Are you—"

"I'd rather not discuss my personal life," he said curtly.

Deep inside him was the hollow ring of derisive laughter. He didn't have a personal life to discuss. His job was his life, because that was the way it had to be. He lived in a sort of vacuum, existing with no emotional entanglements, because emotional entanglements were dangerous to all parties involved. He had learned that lesson in the cruelest way possible.

"I'm sorry," Faith said quietly, not sure where the words had come from. A sudden sense of emptiness ached in her chest as she looked at Shane. The pain was so sharp, it nearly took her breath away.

"Mr. Callan, how seriously are you taking these threats that have been made against Faith?" Alaina asked.

"Considering her value as a witness in the Data-Tech case, we have to take every precaution," Shane said, glad to have something concrete to focus his attention on. "We have every reason to believe

Gerrard and his accomplices will make good on the threats if given the chance."

"The whole thing is ridiculous," Faith grumbled. "William isn't violent; he was only out for the money."

"Well, you would know more about that than I," Shane remarked dryly, his face showing nothing of the unrest inside him. A part of him stubbornly insisted she was guilty. Another part of him wanted to believe in her innocence. And everything male in him simply ached looking at her.

Where had his concentration gone? What had happened to his ability to detach himself emotionally? Faith Kincaid was a job. It made no difference to him if she was guilty or not. So why did he suddenly have this war raging inside him?

He sat back in his chair with a frustrated sigh and reached inside his coat for a cigarette as Jayne and Lindy returned from the kitchen with the pudding.

"Unless you intend on eating your pudding with that cigarette, I'll have to ask you to leave, Mr. Callan," Faith said with as much haughty disdain as she could muster. "This dining room is a smoke-free environment."

Shane stared at her, nonplussed. "You're joking."

"I'm afraid she's not," Alaina said, rising from her chair with a wry smile. "Come along, Mr. Callan. We'll banish ourselves to the front porch."

Outside the evening had turned a darker shade of gray. The lights that flanked the double doors created a small pool of warm light on the porch. Shane automatically shunned it in favor of a darker spot with a sweeping view of the grounds, where he could put his back to the wall and maintain a cautious vigil.

"Where were you practicing law before you came here?" He lit Alaina's cigarette for her and waited for an answer he already knew. Banks had hurriedly scraped up facts on Alaina Montgomery and on Jayne Jordan, a film critic who had been based in LA until two months ago.

"Chicago," she said on a stream of smoke.

"Strange coincidence, isn't it?" Shane lit his own cigarette and took a long, deep pull on it. "That you were living in the same city as DataTech headquarters."

"Life's funny," she said, but her tone held no laughter.

"What made you give up a lucrative practice and move out here?"

"I was burned out."

She wasn't telling him everything, but then he'd known she wouldn't. Alaina was a woman who gave away only what was absolutely necessary, automatically holding facts in reserve. He didn't envy anyone going up against her in a courtroom.

As she looked up at him, Shane recognized something in her direct, measuring gaze—cynicism, wariness; two of his own best friends.

"I didn't ask you out here to discuss the vagaries of fate, Mr. Callan. I want to talk about Faith."

"What about her?"

"I don't want to see her hurt—either by William Gerrard or you."

"Do you want to see her dead?" he asked pointblank. He could see the question confused her for only a split second; then her mind put together the same puzzle pieces his had.

She laughed, seemingly amused by his deduction. Almost admiringly she said, "My, you're a bastard."

"I'm a realist." He picked a fleck of tobacco off his tongue, his eyes never leaving Alaina's. "You came here about the same time Faith did. You obviously ran with a flashy crowd. No reason you couldn't have known the DataTech big shots."

"What's my motive for killing my best friend?" she asked, obviously intrigued by his theory.

"Money is always a nice neat one. Lord knows there's a load of it to be had in the defense contracts game—honestly or otherwise. Greed is a great motivator."

"Don't I know it," Alaina said, a hint of bitterness in her tone.

She was silent for a moment as she finished her cigarette and ground the butt out on the porch railing. She gave Shane a long, measuring look. "My friends and I moved here because we needed a change of scenery. We all came to a crossroads in our lives and decided to take the same new path. I wouldn't hurt Faith or Jayne if you held a gun to my head. We're friends; we care about one another."

"And look out for one another?"

"Faith needs someone to look out for her. In spite of everything she went through with Gerrard, she's too trusting."

"And you're not?"

"No. I don't trust people, and I don't romanticize their motives. If you hurt her, I'll see that you pay for it." She gave him a shrewd smile. "As you guessed, I have some very influential friends."

"Why would I hurt her?" He dismissed her threat. A man who had nothing, had nothing to lose. "I'm here to see she doesn't get hurt."

Alaina's gaze was steady and as cool as the fog that surrounded the house. "Then we won't have a problem, will we?"

Shane tossed his cigarette off the porch as he watched her saunter toward the front door. More amused than angry, he asked, "Who appointed you watchdog?"

She tossed him a saucy look over her shoulder. "It's a self-appointed role. I'm the only Doberman in the pack."

"Somebody should call Clint Eastwood," Jayne said as she carried plates into the kitchen, "to tell him this Callan guy has his voice."

Faith's smile was distracted and halfhearted at best. Jayne gave her a little nudge. "You do it, honey.

I've been on Clint's bad side since I told a few billion people his last movie wasn't worth eating stale popcorn for."

Faith stepped aside from the dishwasher and leaned back against the counter, hugging herself and fighting back tears that had been threatening for hours. She felt as if all her emotions were suddenly ganging up on her, and Jayne's attempt to lighten the mood only made her feel worse.

"Hey," Jayne teased gently, though her eyes were full of concern. "Don't worry about Clint. He'll bounce back."

"I don't think she's upset about Clint," Alaina said as she walked in. "It's our own real-life version of Dirty Harry, isn't it?"

The last subject Faith wanted to discuss was Shane Callan. Nor did she care to go into the strange emotions he drew out of her, charming her one minute and accusing her the next. She decided instead to focus on the reason Callan was there, which was equally unpleasant but easier to understand.

She gave her friends an apologetic look. "I didn't want to involve the two of you in any of this trial business. I'm sorry."

Jayne slid an arm around Faith's shoulders and gave her a reassuring squeeze. "Honey, what's the use in having friends if you can't depend on them in a crisis?"

Alaina crossed her arms in front of her and nodded decisively. "She's right."

"Thanks," Faith murmured, wiping a tear from her lashes.

It had been years since she'd had the solid support of her friends. During her marriage to William she had had no one to depend upon except herself. Now Alaina and Jayne were offering her their shoulders to lean on, and she felt torn between the desire to accept and the ingrained habit of handling her troubles herself.

"I really wanted to believe I'd left everything associated with William behind when I left Washington," she said, shaking her head in dismay. "Now I've got a federal agent skulking around."

"Look on the bright side." Jayne winked at her. "At least he's not hard on the eyes."

That was a fact, Faith thought. It was a fact that made her feel distinctly uneasy. There was something vitally, basically male in Shane Callan that all but reached out and touched the most feminine parts of her. Just the thought of his hard, aristocratic good looks was enough to send heat rushing under her skin. He was making her crazy. What was she doing feeling attracted to the man, knowing what he thought of her?

"He does a hell of a job of fraying nerves, though," Alaina concluded.

Jayne gazed off into space. "He does seem rather hostile, doesn't he? I wonder what motivates that feeling," she said, trying to dissect Shane's performance as if he were a character in a movie. Her brow knitted. "He could be out of touch with his aura."

"Aura my Aunt Sadie." Alaina sniffed. "He's a cop. The attitude is a prerequisite for the job." Dismissing the topic, she turned toward Faith. "Call it a night. Jayne and I can take care of the kitchen. Go read Lindy a bedtime story or something."

Faith turned to dump her leftover onion salad into the trash. "She's already asleep; she wasn't feeling well. Besides, I can't leave you two to handle Robo-Cop alone, when I'm the reason he's here. Where is he anyway?" she asked, swearing to herself it was only idle curiosity that made her ask, not unbridled lust.

"On the porch."

"Shane Callan," Jayne mused dreamily. "With that name and that voice and those looks, it is a crime against humanity that he hasn't found his way to Hollywood."

"I only wish he hadn't found his way here," Faith complained, fanning herself with a pot holder as her hormones threatened to riot.

"Your safety is important," Alaina said, shaking a serving spoon at her. "And not only to the Justice Department. If they think there's some reason to assign you protection, then you ought to accept it."

"They're overreacting," Faith insisted.

"Are they overreacting or are you *under*reacting?" Jayne questioned gently. "Honey, no one could blame you for not wanting to believe your life is in danger."

Faith twisted the pot holder in her hands. "I don't know anymore. The trial is a month away yet. I'd rather not think of it at all, but now I'll be reminded of it every time I turn around and find Eliot Ness watching me as if I'm public enemy number one."

"He's a real piece of work, isn't he?" Jayne gave

a half laugh, then made a stern face and propped her hands on her hips. "Shane Callan—he's not just a man, he's an adventure."

Even Faith managed to laugh. Maybe Jayne was right in trying to find a lighter side to the situation. It was absurd for a federal agent to suspect her of wrongdoing. She was the most ordinary of women. Her needs were simple, she aspired to nothing beyond being a good mother. Yet this cynical, world-weary cop was watching her with an eagle eye. The joke was on Shane Callan.

But Shane Callan wasn't laughing when he burst in the back door of the kitchen. His gun wasn't laughing either. He pressed the nose of it to the head of the frazzled gray-haired man he shoved into the room ahead of him. Faith and Jayne both shrieked and jumped as Callan roughly spun the man around and slammed him back against the kitchen wall, causing three copper molds to clatter to the floor.

"Who the hell are you, and what the hell were you doing under that window?" Shane growled the words in the older man's face.

The old man sputtered right back, though he

was in no position to make demands. "Let me go, ye sly devil!" he ordered in an oddly lilting voice. "Who do ye think ye are, wavin' a gun about!"

Shane's fist wound tighter into the knot of fabric he clutched beneath the man's bearded chin. "I'm the man who's going to make you very unhappy if you don't start answering questions."

The control on Faith's temper snapped like a toothpick when she realized whom Shane was holding at gunpoint. Furious, without a thought as to what Callan's reaction would be, she stormed across the room.

"For Pete's sake, put that gun down before you hurt someone! That's my caretaker you're assaulting, you overgrown bully."

Shane loosened his hold on the man's dirty brown work jacket and half turned to glare at Faith, lowering his pistol as he did so.

"Give me that," she snapped, snatching the gun from his slack hand. "You obnoxious jerk! You can't just bust into my home with guns a-blazing like some kind of reincarnated John Wayne, scaring everybody half to death! You could have given poor Mr. Fitz a heart attack!"

Mr. Fitz stepped away from the wall and his captor, somehow managing to look down his hooked nose at Shane, who stood a head taller. He adjusted his jacket, which reeked of fish, like a king arranging his cloak, then stroked a smoothing hand over his shaggy gray beard.

Shane ignored the old geezer in favor of riveting Faith with a burning look. He was furious with himself for letting her take his gun. What the hell was wrong with him? Was he so off his game he could let a slip of a woman get the drop on him? Or was it just this particular woman, an annoying little voice asked him. He was acting like a green rookie, and it was all Faith Kincaid's fault. He scowled at her.

Suddenly realizing she had his pistol in her hand, she grimaced at it as if it were a slimy dead fish and offered it back to him, holding it pinched between her thumb and forefinger. "Here. Take this awful thing and put it away," she said in her sternest motherly tone. For added oomph she shook her finger at him. "You ought to be ashamed of yourself, pulling a gun on poor Mr. Fitz. He's no killer."

Shane holstered the pistol, an ominous frown pulling his black brows low over his eyes. Lord, she made him feel as if he were ten all over again, in trouble for throwing spit wads in school. "How was I supposed to know that? No one bothered to tell me there was a Mr. Fitz."

Alaina stepped between them, defusing the situation with an introduction as the telephone rang in the background. "Mr. Callan, this is Faith's caretaker, Jack Fitz. Mr. Fitz, this is Agent Callan. The government sent him to keep an eye on Faith because of that trial business."

Mr. Fitz snorted like an infuriated billy goat, his whiskered chin set at a defiant angle. "That better be all ye keep on her, ye big rascal."

Shane rolled his eyes and heaved a much-put-upon sigh. Half under his breath he said, "This place is unbelievable."

"Feel free to go back to Washington to report that," Faith said. She was still seething. She'd had it with him upsetting her household and her nervous system. A quiet life was all she wanted. "You're not welcome here, Mr. Callan. You're not wanted, and you're not needed."

"You've made that first part abundantly clear, Ms. Kincaid," he said, his voice low and silky as he leaned over her.

Faith met his cool, intense stare with one of her own. Shane's look was that of a man who could have stared down the devil himself. Perhaps he had. And underlying the anger that snapped between them like a live wire she could feel a pull, an attraction she neither wanted nor welcomed. A strange tingling raced over her skin as the moment stretched out between them.

"Faith," Jayne called, breaking the tension. "Telephone."

Almost weak with relief, Faith turned away from the confrontation. Her knees wobbled a bit as she crossed the room to take the receiver from Jayne.

"Hello, this is Faith Kincaid."

"How would you like to be dead, Mrs. Gerrard?" a man's voice questioned very softly.

Blinding, instantaneous fear lodged in Faith's throat. She felt as if she had suddenly been encased in ice, and yet her palms were sweating as she clutched the receiver to her ear. The only thing she could think to say was ridiculous, but she said it anyway, her voice shot through with trembling threads of panic. "Who is this?"

"A friend," the man answered, but there was nothing friendly in his voice; it held all the silky menace of a viper, dark and evil. "A friend who thinks it would be better if you didn't testify, because I'd hate to have to kill you."

For a long moment Faith listened to the silence after the soft click on the other end of the line. Finally she hung up and turned slowly to face the other people in the room. If she had felt weak before the call, she felt faint now, and she knew she had turned as white as the kitchen appliances. She was certain no one could feel as cold and terrified as she did and still have a red blood cell left in her body.

Everyone in the room stared at her, their faces grim with worry. They seemed miles away, even though they were in the same room.

She didn't turn to her friends. Her gaze went directly, instinctively to Shane Callan and locked on him desperately, as if she could somehow draw strength from merely looking at him. Faith didn't question her reaction; fear had stripped away the ability to question and reason.

Managing to draw a shaky breath into her lungs, she said, "It would seem I was a bit hasty in saying you aren't needed here."

THREE

HE COULDN'T SLEEP. No matter how hard he tried, no matter how detached he claimed to be, he couldn't blank the image from his mind. Every time he closed his eyes all he could see was Faith Kincaid, looking small and terrified, her face washed of color, her dark eyes staring up at him, wide and shining with tears of fear.

She had looked to him in that instant, and his first and strongest instinct had been to take her in his arms and hold her.

Shane swore softly, exhaling a stream of smoke

toward the ceiling. What the hell was the matter with him?

Lurking not so far in the back of his mind was the fear that after sixteen years on the job, maybe it was time to move on to something else. But when he tried to see the future, it simply stretched before him, a barren gray plain. His dedication to duty had distanced him from everyone and everything he had ever cared about. Now he had nothing to move on to.

Without turning on the light he sat up and reached for the tumbler on the nightstand and took a swallow of velvet-smooth whiskey.

Banks had wanted him to take R and R after the Silvanus case. Correction, Shane thought with a wry smile, as he took another long drag on his cigarette, Banks had *ordered* him to take R and R after the Silvanus case. He probably should have listened. Instead, he'd picked one hell of a fight with his boss, and now he was stuck here. This was Banks's way of punishing him. When Shane thought of the woman lying in bed just across the hall from him, and his blood surged hot in his veins, he had to say it was cruel and unusual punishment.

What a pretty little bundle of trouble Faith Kincaid was. In the first place he wanted to believe she was as guilty as her ex-husband where DataScam was concerned. That alone should have kept him from feeling this damnable attraction. Under the tarnish of cynicism he was still a patriot. And if she really was as innocent as those big brown eyes of hers claimed, she was a civilian under his protection. That meant hands off.

But, oh, how he'd wanted to touch her when she had hung up that phone and turned to him. He had felt every facet of her fear, had known she was looking to him for strength, for protection. The protection she had been so certain she didn't need.

Shane told himself his job was keeping Faith safe and sound until the trial. He had men stationed at strategic points on the property, well hidden from view. Tomorrow Del Matthews would arrive to tap the phones. They would construct a safety net around Faith, hoping to catch whoever was after her rather than simply frighten them away.

He stubbed his cigarette out in the little porcelain dish that was intended for bedtime mints and rubbed the back of his neck. Everything was under control. Repeating that in his head, he lay back down on the rumpled sheets and tried to relax. Everything was under control.

Everything had been under control in the Silvanus case. All the players in the Silvanus operation were now either dead or under indictment. Except Strauss. It haunted Shane that the most lethal of Silvanus's cohorts had escaped, but that case was over. Here and now, everything was under control.

Everything had been under control at Quantico ten years ago too. Still, Ellie was dead.

Cold swept over him in a sheen of damp sweat. Where had that memory come from? He had buried it along with Ellie. Why had it surfaced now?

The image of Faith Kincaid floated through his mind, but Shane stubbornly ignored the clue and hauled himself out of bed to pace naked back and forth across the width of the small room. With a strength of will few men possessed, he pushed the memories out of his mind. This wasn't Quantico. Nobody was going to get to Faith Kincaid because it was his job to keep her safe. End of story.

As those words branded themselves in his mind, a sound penetrated his thoughts, snatching hold of his attention. It was faint, overhead on the second

or third floor, but it was distinct. Ker-thump...
ker-thump...ker-thump...

Hastily he pulled on a pair of pants, grabbed his
gun, and slipped from the room.

She couldn't sleep. She couldn't begin to relax,
not even after her friends had forced a glass of
brandy on her. The one instant she had finally
begun to doze off she had been awakened by an
itching sensation on her chest where the pendant
of her necklace lay.

Great. Not only were there killers after her, she
was developing an allergy as well, Faith thought,
as she sat up and switched the bedside lamp on.

In the soft light she studied the delicate gold fili-
gree heart as she often did. The intricate lacework
of the piece had always enchanted her. When
Bryan had given her the necklace as a graduation
present, he had claimed there was magic in it. Of
course, for her friend Bryan Hennessy there was
magic in everything. Where was the magic now,
Faith wondered, now that she and Lindy were in
danger.

Trembling, she pulled the covers up even though

she wasn't cold. She had felt so safe here. All it had taken to shatter that sense of well-being was a phone call. That easily, evil had violated her home, her peace. The overwhelming sense of vulnerability that swept through her at the thought was frightening. And with the helplessness came anger. She had always taken care of her own problems. This was one she couldn't begin to handle on her own.

Shane Callan, a presence she had wanted removed from her life earlier in the day, had suddenly become her savior. It made little sense. She hardly knew him, yet she had immediately turned to him. The whole episode had taken on a surrealistic quality in her memory. Had she really seen concern in his translucent gray eyes, or had she imagined it? Had she imagined the softer quality in his low voice as he had questioned her, or had that been genuine?

All she was really certain of was that her world had been turned upside down yet again. How could such an ordinary person find herself constantly thrown into extraordinary circumstances, she wondered. She was just a girl from the farm country of Ohio. What did she know of spies and assassins?

Needing to do something that was comforting in its normalcy, she tossed the covers aside, slipped out of bed, and padded barefoot across the rug to the door that connected her room to Lindy's. She looked in on her daughter and frowned. Lindy was tossing and turning too, but at least she was asleep. Faith doubted she was going to get any rest at all.

She pulled a light blue robe on over her nightgown and quietly slipped out of her room, intending to go to the library to find something to read. Then she heard it. Ker-thump...ker-thump...ker-thump...

"Never misses a night," she murmured, a faint smile turning her lips.

Instead of going to the library, she turned and crept up the grand staircase.

She barely glimpsed the dark figure that bolted out from behind the drapes flanking the Palladian window on the second-floor landing. Before she could scream, she found herself pressed back against the wall with a large hand clamped over her mouth, a gun pressed to her temple, and a hard male body pressed along the length of her. Terror surged through her, pebbling the texture of her skin and drawing her nipples into tight knots.

"What the hell are you doing here?" Shane uttered the words through clenched teeth. He slid his hand from her mouth to the wall beside her head. His eyes looked cold and silvery in the moonlight that fell through the arched window.

Faith pulled a shaking breath into her lungs. "This *is* my house," she whispered. "I'm free to roam it at will, aren't I?"

"That depends on why you're roaming."

She made a face. There was no way he was going to believe her if she told him the truth, so she settled on half of it. "I couldn't sleep. What's your excuse?"

"I don't need one."

Faith frowned at him. "You're an absolute menace, sneaking around, manhandling people, holding that awful gun to their heads. You're liable to end up killing somebody."

Shane never took his eyes off her as he tucked his pistol into the back of his pants. Nor did he move, keeping her pinned against the wall with his own weight. She was soft against him, trembling. Her nipples seemed to burn him through the sheer silky fabric of her nightgown.

Anger swelled inside him, right along with desire. Dammit, she was trouble. He could keep only half his mind on the job. The other half was preoccupied savoring the feel of her against him, wondering what it would be like to have her warm and willing beneath him. He had to fight to keep from staring at her sweet, full mouth just inches below his.

"Who am I liable to kill up here?" he asked. "No one has a room in this part of the house... unless there's someone else you neglected to mention to me. Is there, Faith?"

"No," she murmured.

Why didn't he back off and give her some room? Being wedged between the wall and his body was having a devastating effect on her mind. Her eyes kept drifting to the bare width of his shoulders and chest. A sculptor couldn't have carved a more artistic representation of the male animal. His muscles flexed and rippled in the moonlight. A square pad of white gauze was taped to his left shoulder, but it didn't detract from his masculine beauty; it only emphasized the fact that he was a dangerous man.

"Then there's nothing to worry about if I decide to go upstairs, is there?" he said.

Faith felt she had plenty to worry about—the coil of desire tightening inside her, the feel of Shane's rock-hard thighs imprisoning her, the fact that she seemed to want to stare at the sharp, firm lines of his mouth. At the moment she was more afraid of this immediate threat than the one she had received over the phone.

"No," she whispered, not certain whether she was answering his question or denying the sudden ache of needs long neglected.

"No," Shane echoed, very aware of what he was denying. He could feel himself growing heavy and hard against the pillow of Faith's body as she stared at his mouth. It was a toss-up as to whether he was angrier with her for tempting him or with himself for knowing he was about to give in to that temptation.

"There's nothing to worry about," he said in a low, rough voice, "unless this is what you came looking for."

It was more an assault than a kiss. Shane's mouth slanted across Faith's, angry and demanding. His fingertips dug into her shoulders, pulling her even more firmly against his bare chest. She bent back like an archer's bow under the pressure, her hips arching into his in a way that made his state of arousal very apparent.

Faith's first instinct was to get away from him, but that response was almost immediately overtaken by another, more powerful instinct she seemed to have no control over—the instinct to give in to him. The desire was so strong that she sagged against him and her lips softened beneath his, allowing his tongue access to her mouth. Pure fire seared her veins at the intimate invasion, at the heady taste of him.

When Shane's right hand slipped inside her open robe to cup her breast, she nearly cried out, the pleasure was so intense. His long fingers explored her through the silky fabric of her gown, his thumb flicking across the nipple that was already hard and aching. All the while his tongue plunged and receded in the warmth of her mouth, his message more than clear. He wanted her.

He wanted her. He didn't respect her. He didn't

seem particularly fond of her. In fact, he had insinuated she was a criminal.

Then what in the world was she doing kissing him, Faith asked herself as common sense returned in a painful rush. It was accompanied by a sharp dose of self-loathing. What was wrong with her that she could feel attracted to this man who thought so little of her? Lord, he had all but said she'd come upstairs looking for this!

Tearing her mouth from beneath his, she jerked out of his arms and slapped him hard. The sound was like a shot in the still of the night. Shane stared at her, his expression a mix of anger, surprise, and thwarted passion.

Faith cursed herself again at the rush of desire she felt looking at him. He was only half-dressed. With his black hair tousled and his features outlined in the moonlight, he looked like an elegant savage.

"What's the matter, Faith?" he asked, his voice a menacing, silky purr. "Isn't seducing a federal agent in your repertoire?"

His sarcasm cut her to the quick. She took a step back and started to turn, ready to run to the sanctuary of her room, but she stopped herself.

Who did he think he was, accusing her of wrongs she hadn't committed, pushing her around in her own home, taking advantage of her and then blaming her for it? No more. She wasn't going to put up with one more insult. When she had left William, she had vowed never to let another man manipulate or use her again. It was time to honor that vow.

"I've had it with you and your sarcastic insinuations," she began. "Who are you to judge me? You don't know anything about me except what bare facts you read in some file. Well, here are a few more facts for you, Mr. Callan.

"William Gerrard married me because he thought I would be good for his image. I stayed with him because I was fool enough to believe I could change him. But he was a cold, unfeeling son of a bitch, just like you. He used me when I fit his needs and ignored me the rest of the time. And when I accidentally found out what he was up to with the DataTech people, I left him, because I couldn't keep a vow to a man who cheated on both his wife and his country.

"I went to the Justice Department because I believed it was the right thing to do, not because I was trying to protect myself from prosecution.

I haven't done anything wrong." Tears flowed freely down her cheeks, and she reached up to wipe them away, never taking her eyes off Shane. Her mouth trembled, but she held her chin at a stubborn, defiant angle, refusing to back down from him. "The only crime I committed was believing William Gerrard ever loved me."

Shane looked away, raising a hand to rub the back of his neck, his own anger thoroughly doused by shame. She was telling the truth. He could hear it. Her voice rang with it. He could see it in her eyes. It cut through the barrier of his cynicism and made him face the fact that he had wanted her to be guilty because it was easier for him to deal with lies and deception than with innocence. Lord, what had he become?

"I wanted my husband to love me. What's the penalty for that, Mr. Callan?" she asked him in a voice soft with tears and pain. She sniffed and added on a bitter note, "Besides having to put up with you, I mean."

"That seems to be punishment enough," he murmured, turning to stare out the window.

Fog obscured the view, but he didn't really care. In his mind's eye all he could see was Faith standing there in her silky nightgown, her bare toes peeking out from under the hem, her full breasts rising and falling with each jerky breath, her eyes shining with tears, her mouth swollen from the kiss he had forced on her.

Glancing down, he could clearly see the imprint of her heart pendant on the skin of his chest where he had all but crushed her against him. His cheek still stung from the slap she'd given him, but it didn't burn in quite the same way as the mark on his chest did.

Once upon a time he had been a man of honor and principles. Somewhere along the way he had stopped believing in innocence. He had submerged himself in a gray world where there were only the guilty and the less guilty. And his strongest motivation had become staying alive so he could put the worst of the lot behind bars.

Faith Kincaid wasn't a part of that world, but when he turned to tell her so, she was gone.

"I'm not being a coward," Faith mumbled to herself as she fussed with Lindy's covers.

Her daughter had dropped off to sleep. There

was really no reason for Faith to sit by the bed. Lindy had come down with a normal case of childhood chicken pox, not malaria. Now would have been the perfect opportunity to slip out for a while and get a few things accomplished in the house. Still, she lingered, as she had lingered all morning.

No matter how many times she told herself otherwise, she knew she was avoiding Shane. She had spent the night alternately reliving their kiss and reliving her fury. Much of her anger had been directed at herself for that brief moment when she had surrendered to him and her own desire. Shame burned in her cheeks every time she thought about it. This time, though, she headed it off at the pass.

What did she have to be ashamed of? It was Shane's fault. He had taken advantage of her when she had been startled and confused. She had no reason to hide from him. This was her home. She was going to have to put up with him skulking around, but she'd be damned if she was going to jump behind a door every time she saw him coming.

Her resolve sufficiently bolstered, Faith marched to the bedroom door and stepped out into the hall—directly into the path of Shane Callan. His arms went around her in an automatic reaction to save her from falling. The contact of body against body was brief, and yet Faith felt as if she had run directly into the sun, the heat was so intense. Sexual awareness exploded through her, shattering her sense of calm into a million shards.

"I'm sorry," Shane mumbled. He felt knocked off balance. Not by Faith's slight weight, but by the instantaneous rush of feeling their collision had brought on. It overrode even the burning pain in his shoulder. He shook his head to clear it, then fixed his gaze just to the left of Faith's head.

Business. They had things to discuss that had nothing to do with the way she felt in his arms. "I need to speak with you about certain aspects of the surveillance. Agent Matthews has arrived to tap the phones. He'll need an operations base, and I would prefer it be outside the main house. The caretaker's cottage would be ideal."

"You'll have to take that up with Mr. Fitz. He owns the cottage outright," Faith said, struggling not to notice how sleekly handsome he looked in navy trousers and a blue striped dress shirt, a silk tie neatly knotted beneath his square chin.

She knew for a fact that she looked like a bag lady. She hadn't gotten a moment's sleep and had been waiting on Lindy since before dawn. Her clothes were rumpled, her hair looked like a squirrel's nest. It irked her that Shane didn't seem to notice, and it irked her that she cared.

"We also need a list of the guests you've booked in advance as well as a list of any household help you've hired," he went on.

Faith pinched the bridge of her nose and sighed. "You're going to check them all out? It was a man who called. With the exception of Mr. Fitz all the help I've hired are women."

"That doesn't mean they couldn't be connected in some way. Someone had to tell him where you are."

"Do what you have to," Faith said tiredly, wishing with all her might she could just close her eyes and will all this mess away.

Something in Shane ached at her expression. She looked so small and fragile...and innocent. He cursed himself again for having been such a bastard toward her. Her life was complicated enough right now without having the man who was supposed to protect her harassing her as well.

He cleared his throat in a rare show of nerves.

What the hell did he know about relating to a woman like Faith? "Um—how's Lindy? Ms. Jordan mentioned she'd come down with something."

Faith shrugged, glad for the change of subject and touched by his show of concern. "She's resting for the moment. She's uncomfortable. I'm sure you remember how it was to have the chicken pox."

"Actually, no. I never had them."

"Figures," Faith mumbled.

"Faith." Apologizing was something he'd never been good at. The words stuck in his throat like peanut butter. "About last night, I—"

"I think we said everything that needed saying." Her voice was a little shaky, but she managed to look him square in the eye as she took another step back from him.

"Mama?" Lindy's voice drifted out from her room.

"If you'll excuse me, Agent Callan, my daughter needs me."

Shane nodded, sighing in frustration as Faith went back into Lindy's room. Maybe it would be for the best if he let her go on thinking he was an obnoxious jerk. Ordinarily the opinion of others mattered little to him. He conducted himself as he saw fit, and to hell with the rest of the world. But it bothered him that he had treated her badly. Deep down, in a place inside him no person had touched in a very long time, it mattered what Faith Kincaid thought about him.

Swearing under his breath, he stalked off down the hall.

It just wouldn't do for him to become attached to her in any way, and still he could feel the pull, the attraction. He had felt it the instant he'd first seen her, even though he had believed she was involved in the DataTech scam. Now that he knew she wasn't, the desire was only going to be stronger.

He'd lain awake imagining what it would be like to go into her room and take her gently in his arms, to hold her and kiss her fears away. Every inch of his body had throbbed as he'd thought of what it would be like to make love to her until she forgot she'd ever known William Gerrard. And he had cursed himself to hell and gone for being so foolish. Faith Kincaid was a job. For both their sakes she could be nothing more.

———

Shane wandered through the halls of the big silent house, trying to unwind. In one hand he cradled a snifter of cognac, the other hand he stuffed into his trouser pocket. His shoulder throbbed with hot, sharp pain that defied mere aspirin. He was bone tired, as if he had spent the day doing hard physical labor under a hot sun. And yet an aching restlessness snaked through him, keeping him from falling into his bed.

The situation was well in hand. After a royal battle with the querulous Mr. Fitz, Matthews had gotten set up in the caretaker's cottage. The phones were tapped. The other agents were in place and inconspicuous. Background checks were being conducted on all inn employees, including the cantankerous Jack Fitz. All he had to do now was wait... and watch Faith.

He had seen little of her after their encounter in the hallway. Shane told himself that was for the best. Yet he had found himself at Lindy's door not five minutes earlier, checking to see if Faith would speak to him. It seemed what was left of his conscience was bent on apologizing to her. He just had to remember not to let it go any further than that.

He had found her asleep, propped up against the headboard of Lindy's narrow bed with one arm wrapped protectively around her sleeping child. Mother and child asleep in the golden glow from a small lamp with a teddy-bear base. The scene had easily, effortlessly breached Shane's defenses and left an ache near his heart.

His world was so remote from theirs. Now, for a short time, their paths would cross. Then he would go on alone into the gray shadows. The thought left him feeling hollow. Hollow and so alone.

Without turning on a light, he crossed the polished wood floor of the ballroom to the grand piano that sat in the far corner, moonlight spilling across it through the large windows. He set his glass down and flipped on the brass light that illuminated the keyboard. Then he sat down and began to play, the music flowing from his memory and his soul.

Faith awoke suddenly from a sound sleep. She scratched absently at the place where her heart charm lay against her skin as she looked down on Lindy.

Lotion and baths with baking soda added to the water had soothed her daughter's itching enough to let her sleep peacefully for a few hours. Her fever was down. Luckily her case of chicken pox wasn't very severe.

Careful not to wake her, Faith eased herself off the bed and went to the door, stretching cramped muscles. When she stepped out into the hall, she stopped and listened.

Music. It was faint, but she was immediately stricken by the poignancy of the piece. Every note was filled with longing, with an aching tenderness. The passage swelled with the pain of dreams unfulfilled. Loneliness hung in the silences between the notes.

She followed the sound to the door of the ballroom. Her heart lodged in her throat as she leaned against the doorjamb. Shane sat at the keyboard of the piano, his fingers caressing the ivory keys with the care of a lover. He played with his eyes closed, his face pale in the glow of the piano light. And she could see in his expression every emotion she heard in his music.

The song went on, slow and sad, rising and

falling, wrapping itself around her, drawing her into its sensual web. Faith's eyes filled with tears. Whatever she had chosen to think of Shane Callan, she couldn't discount what she was hearing now. He was a lonely, haunted man. Those feelings reached out to her and penetrated her soul. They filled her with a sense of abject emptiness so sharp, she nearly cried out from it.

She knew nothing about him. What she had seen thus far hadn't been Shane, but his defenses. She realized it in a blinding flash, and the knowledge both comforted and terrified her. Knowing there was more to him than cynicism and machismo didn't change the fact that he was a dangerous man.

His fingers slowed on the keys as the piece softened to its close, a low minor chord that echoed in the still room.

"That was lovely," Faith said, her voice hushed with reverence.

Shane looked up, startled that she had been able to approach without him knowing it. He was startled too by how lovely she seemed, He couldn't figure out why. She was wearing jeans and a blue sweatshirt that was much too large for her. Her clothes were rumpled. Her mop of rusty blond curls was in complete disarray, looking as if an impatient lover had run his fingers through the mass over and over.

Perhaps this was how she would look after making love—tousled, a rosy blush tinting the apples of her cheeks, her dark eyes sleepy. A fresh wave of heat swept over him at the thought.

Suddenly aware he was staring, he caught himself. Damn, he felt as awkward as an untried kid. Squelching the feeling, he said, "I hope I didn't wake you."

Faith shook her head, then amazed herself by sitting down beside him on the bench. She faced the opposite direction, her thigh no more than an inch or two from his. It seemed tantamount to going into a cage to lie down beside a panther. But somehow, after hearing his music, she felt less wary of him. He didn't look like a man to be frightened of now. He looked tired and bleary-eyed and lonely. If that was how he felt, then they had a lot in common.

"How's Lindy?"

"She'll be back to herself in a day or so." She folded her hands on her lap to keep from fidgeting. "Is everything . . . in place?"

"Yes. Now we wait for him to make the next move."

She shivered at the prospect of receiving another threatening call. Every time she let her guard down, she could hear the ugly menace beneath the silky, faceless voice that had promised death.

Unable to stop himself, Shane lifted a hand and brushed back a curl from her cheek. "He won't get to you. I won't let him."

"I don't mean to be a coward," she whispered, trying hard to ignore the warmth of his knuckles against her skin. She told herself she had imagined the possessive tone of his words. She was romanticizing again. "This all just seems so ... unreal."

Shane nodded. He imagined it did seem unreal to her. The threat of death was something that belonged in his world, not hers. Chicken pox and pot roast should have been the extent of her worries. "You're no coward," he said. "I think you're very brave."

"A compliment?" She had to force the smile, but the surprise in her eyes was genuine, and so was the warmth that blossomed in her heart. "I didn't know you had it in you."

"Oh, I'm full of surprises," Shane said with a wry, weary grin that made him look devilishly handsome. "Not all of them are unpleasant."

Faith said nothing but rubbed her pendant absently between her thumb and forefinger as she looked down at the floor. He was full of surprises all right, just like Pandora's box. And like the girl in the story, Faith knew an irresistible urge to open the box. Not smart, Faith, she told herself.

"You realize now you have no choice but to delay the opening of the inn."

"I know. I'll call everyone and tell them the plumbing isn't ready. Nothing puts people off quite like the thought of malfunctioning commodes."

Shane chuckled, ignoring the throbbing it set off in his head. He was surprised Faith had any sense of humor left. She'd been threatened and bullied and run ragged over the last couple of days, yet she seemed to have a reservoir of inner strength to call on when she needed it. There was a hell of a lot more to the former Mrs. William Gerrard than met the eye. And what met the eye held a lot more appeal than it should have.

"Faith," he began, fighting the urge to touch her

again. He was beginning to have trouble concentrating on anything other than the delicate shape of her mouth and the memory of how sweet she had tasted. He had to apologize now, just get it over with and get away from her. "I was out of line last night. I had no right to accuse you of anything. I've seen the worst side of people for so long, I guess I've just come to expect it. I'm sorry."

"First a compliment, now an apology." Faith shook her head. "Really, Mr. Callan, you're making me giddy," she said, teasing lights sparkling in her dark eyes as she fanned herself with her hand.

"Is the apology accepted?"

She nodded but didn't look at him. Was he apologizing only for his belief in her culpability or for the kiss as well?

Overhead the sound began. Ker-thump . . . ker-thump . . . ker-thump . . .

Shane tensed. Faith smiled. "It's Captain Dugan."

He stared at her as if she'd suddenly begun speaking Portuguese. "Who?"

"The man who built the place."

"He's dead." His statement held all the finality of the fact.

Faith rolled her eyes. "I know that. It's his ghost. Ask anyone in Anastasia. They'll all tell you the same thing. This house is haunted."

"Californians," Shane grumbled, scowling darkly.

"Skeptic," Faith countered. A man like Shane Callan wouldn't believe in anything that couldn't be admitted as evidence in a court of law. She suddenly found the trait oddly endearing and decided she was losing her marbles. "Of course it's Captain Dugan. He had a peg leg. The other ghosts here don't make any racket at all."

Shane's brows lifted. No one had warned him he would be guarding a crazy woman. "Other ghosts?"

Faith's look was one of feminine wisdom and mystery. "You don't believe in ghosts, do you, Mr. Callan?"

Not the kind that haunted houses, he thought. He knew well the ghosts that haunted one's soul were all too real, but dead sea captains with peg legs were a whole different thing.

He frowned at Faith as he rose from the piano bench, his head swimming as he did so. He ignored the dizziness as he had all day. It was nothing more than fatigue.

Easing his gun from its holster, he said dryly, "I believe in justice, football, and Smith and Wesson. Go to your room, lock your door, and stay put."

Faith shook her head as she watched him leave. Of all the cops in the world she had to get stuck with Dirty Harry. And darn it, she had a terrible feeling she was falling for him.

FOUR

"THE STRESS IS making you irrational," Faith muttered to herself as she paced the width of her bedroom. "That's the only logical explanation. You're not really falling for Shane Callan."

Her entire body seemed to reject the statement she'd just made. An ominous sense of certainty descended on her.

She had to admit the physical attraction had been there from the beginning, from the minute she'd opened the front door and looked up into his silver eyes, from the instant she'd first heard his sexy bedroom voice. She hadn't been able to deny it even when he had all but accused her of treason.

Lust. There wasn't anything rational or logical about it.

But this was more than mere lust.

Faith's slim shoulders rose and fell with her sigh of defeat. She couldn't have picked a more difficult man if she had held auditions for the part. Shane was jaded, sardonic, a loner...he was battered and tired and alone. Just the memory of him sitting at the piano, pouring out feelings he would never have revealed otherwise, brought a pang to Faith's heart. There were no two ways about it—the darn man needed love.

"But I don't have to be the one to give it to him," she declared with a shake of her head, half wishing he'd never apologized to her for suspecting she was in on the DataTech conspiracy.

At least before his apology his suspicion had been an effective barrier between them. Now that wall was gone. Now Faith knew there was a lot more to Shane than what pleasingly met the eye. Now she was in real peril.

She had a wealth of love inside her, stored up

from years of being married to a man who had looked on her as nothing more than an asset. But she knew she would have to be a fool to try to give those feelings to a man like Shane.

Shane Callan was a dangerous stranger, there because it was his job to protect her. Their lives would run on the same track only until the DataScam trial. In a matter of weeks Shane would be gone to fight someone else's battles. To become involved with him would only be asking to have her heart broken.

No, Faith announced inwardly, she wouldn't make that mistake. She had settled there to rebuild her life, not to tear it apart all over again.

A knock at her door jolted her from her brooding. Alaina stuck her head in the room. "I just got in and saw your light. Is something going on?"

Faith rolled her eyes. "Rambo is upstairs trying to hunt down Captain Dugan."

Alaina's wry smile tilted up one side of her lush mouth as she came in and closed the door behind her. "I don't suppose it did you any good to explain to him about the captain?"

"A complete waste of good breath. The man has

a head harder than granite." And the rest of him wasn't exactly Play-Doh, either. The thought sneaked into her conscious mind from her memory, bringing a telltale flush to her cheeks.

"He's not the type to believe in things he can't point a gun at," Alaina said.

Like love and romance. Faith cursed her brain for letting thoughts like that form and surface. She resumed her pacing, hoping the movement, coupled with the dim light in the room, would keep Alaina from reading too much in her expression. Her friend had an uncomfortably sharp eye when it came to reading people.

"Well." Alaina shrugged, sticking her hands in the pockets of her red cashmere cardigan. "He'll find out for himself that there's nothing up there worth arresting. He can't very well slap handcuffs on an apparition. How's Lindy? Still itching?"

Faith smiled in appreciation for the change of subject. Her whole body relaxed visibly as she leaned against the carved cherry foot post of her canopied bed. "She's much better tonight. This might be the world's easiest case of chicken pox, which means I have something to be grateful for after all. How was the movie?"

It was Alaina's turn to roll her eyes. "Let me give you a piece of sound advice," she said, prowling the small bedroom as if it were a courtroom and Faith a juror who needed to hear a convincing argument. Her elegant hands moved in harmony to emphasize her words. "Never go to the movies with a film critic. Our dear friend Jayne, whom I find to be perfectly pleasant in most respects, is a fanatic. She takes her vocation much too seriously."

"She didn't like the movie?"

"*Roget's Thesaurus* doesn't hold as many synonyms for the word bad," Alaina said dryly.

As if summoned, a head of rich auburn waves poked into the room. "Is there something exciting going on?"

On cue a thud sounded overhead. Alaina grinned and motioned her inside. "You'll love this. Callan is upstairs playing ghostbusters."

"Bad casting," Jayne said, making a face as she slipped into the room and shut the door behind her. "I have serious doubts about Faith's Mr. Callan playing comedy. He doesn't seem particularly fun loving. My guess is he's a Capricorn."

"He's not *my* Mr. Callan." Faith protested so quickly the words seemed to tumble over each other on their way out of her mouth. She looked on in horror as her friends exchanged a significant glance. "I mean, he's here because of me, but I don't *want* him. I mean, I don't want him *here*. Not that I'd want him *anywhere*."

She groaned under her breath and knocked her forehead against the bedpost. She'd just managed to make it fairly obvious that she was attracted to the man. She jumped as Jayne's hand settled gently on her shoulder.

"Honey, if you'd ever care to translate that into understandable English, I'd be more than willing to listen." Jayne shot a questioning look at Alaina, who physically backed away from the topic.

"Don't look at me for advice on this. I'm a lawyer. I'm the last person you want to talk to about romance, unless it concerns community property."

"No," Faith said dejectedly. "Shane Callan is the last person I want to talk to about romance. The man wears a gun strapped to his ankle, for heaven's sake! I saw it when he was tying his shoe. A gun! That's not the kind of thing that fits readily into my lifestyle. That's something that should be in a movie!"

"It was," Jayne said earnestly. She poked her hands into the patch pockets of her wildly flowered dress. "Didn't you see *Deadly Justice*?"

"No."

"Just as well. The script sucked swamp water."

Faith shook her head, both to clear it and to get her thoughts back on track. Jayne was infamous for losing the thread of a conversation. In another few sentences she could have them discussing metaphysics.

"I can't afford to be attracted to a man like Shane Callan," Faith announced, as if saying it aloud could steel her resolve.

An authoritative knock sounded at the door. Without waiting for an invitation, the object of her dismay stepped inside the bedroom, his expression that of a thwarted hunter. He directed his ferocious frown at Faith.

"I told you to lock the door."

"It doesn't have a lock," Faith said, shrugging, as she pushed herself away from her bed. She knew his sense of caution was for her own safety, but she hated the idea of having to be a virtual prisoner in her own home. Dryly she said, "I was about to push the dresser in front of it when Jayne and Alaina came in."

"We're not armed, honey, and we're only slightly dangerous," Jayne assured him with a wink.

Shane scowled at her and holstered his pistol, wincing at the pressure the wide leather strap exerted against his aching shoulder. It felt like a branding iron burning into his sensitive flesh. He managed to ignore both the pain and his blurring vision. "After that phone call I'd think you'd be taking this business seriously."

"We are, Mr. Callan," Alaina said, stepping forward to defend her friends. "We're just trying to make the best of a bad situation."

Suddenly feeling weak, he let the subject drop as he leaned back against the door. Once again his gaze fell on Faith, who stood beside her bed. Desire stirred through the haze of pain. Desire to stretch out with her on cool crisp sheets and feel her small soft hands on his fevered skin. Her eyes widened slightly as she took in his predatory expression.

"You didn't find anything, did you?" she blurted out, crossing her arms to keep her hands from fidgeting.

Don't let him see he makes you nervous, she thought, then groaned inwardly. Lord, Faith, he's a man, not a charging rhinoceros. Besides, she was fairly certain he wouldn't have come running had she announced she was having hopelessly romantic notions about him. At the moment his mind was occupied with things other than the mysteries of biological attraction.

Shane took in the feminine decor of the room in a narrow-eyed glance, not answering. He hated to admit defeat. He had followed thumping noises all over the upstairs of the main house and not gotten so much as a glimpse of the cause. Every time he'd thought he'd cornered the culprit, the thump had sounded three rooms away.

It irked the hell out of him. If only he weren't so damned tired. If only he could clear the fuzz out of his brain, he was sure he could have figured out what was going on up there. At the moment he didn't believe he could figure out two plus two.

"No." The word was the next best thing to a growl. "I didn't find anything, but that doesn't mean there wasn't anything up there."

Faith nearly chuckled at the disgruntled scowl

that tugged down his straight black brows and the corners of his mouth. She gave him a smug smile, unable to resist. "I told you so."

"I'm not about to swallow that ghost story," he declared. He started to lift his left hand to wag a finger at her, but the pain in his shoulder stopped him. He gritted his teeth against it as it rocketed through his chest and arm, and he leaned back against the door again to steady himself.

"We have a friend who is a psychic investigator who could no doubt explain it to you better than I," Faith said, trying to imagine Shane Callan and Bryan Hennessy embroiled in a debate over paranormal phenomena. "But he's working in Britain right now, and the best I can do is tell you in plain English—this house is haunted."

Jayne plopped down cross-legged on the pink-and-cream-colored quilt that covered Faith's bed, her voluminous skirt billowing around her. "You should talk to Mr. Fitz about it. He's full of ghost stories about this place."

Shane scowled harder at mention of the irascible old caretaker. "Ghost stories aren't the only thing he's full of, nor are they what I want to hear."

"I can't offer another explanation," Faith said.

"You've been through the whole house. Your men have been watching it constantly. No one could have gotten in."

"Unless they had help from inside."

Alaina shook her head as his cool gray gaze settled on her. "We've had this conversation before."

He turned to Jayne, who started in surprise at his suspicion. "Don't look at me, honey! I don't even like violence in film. I'm a firm believer in the transcendental rise of man above his baser physical nature."

Shane opened his mouth to comment, but Faith cut him off with a friendly warning. "Shane, please, stop accusing my friends."

"It's my job," he said, exasperated by her overabundance of blind trust.

"Well, you're very good at it. The only person who's managed to escape your jaundiced eye is Lindy."

Shane did a better job of ignoring her sarcasm than he did of ignoring the way her crossed arms lifted her breasts. The womanly mounds plumped together beneath the fabric of her sweatshirt, the outline of hard nipples clearly indicating she wore no bra.

Business, Shane, he told himself. Strictly business.

"What about secret passages? Have you found any as you've been working on the house?"

The man was remarkable. "Who do we look like, Charlie's Angels?" Faith asked. "I'm opening the place as an inn, not a spook house."

"You're the one going on about ghosts," Shane grumbled. He rubbed at the incessant pounding in his right temple. Damn, but his head was feeling fuzzy. He barely heard Faith's next words through the thick, cotton-wool fog that enveloped his brain.

"We have them." She shrugged, knowing she probably wouldn't have been able to convince Shane had Captain Dugan materialized at her side that very moment, peg leg and all. "What can I say?"

Shane pushed himself away from the door, his legs feeling as thick and heavy as tree trunks. The puzzle would have to wait until morning to be solved. He couldn't think anymore. Damned if he was going to be able to move. He had to find a place to sit down for a couple of minutes.

Faith's heart lurched as she realized how pale he looked. His face had gone as white as the apparitions he refused to believe in. Alarm streaked through her as he took another step and dropped like a rock at her feet.

"We've got to get him to the hospital. Jayne, go call the ambulance."

"No. No ambulance. We can't attract the attention. The whole case will be shot to hell."

"Damn your case!"

Shane could hear the conversation going on above him. He recognized the voices as those of agent Del Matthews and Faith Kincaid. Del sounded unflappable. Faith sounded frantic. They both sounded far away.

He tried to rouse the strength to stand, but his body was nothing more than dead weight, oblivious to the commands of his considerable will. He couldn't even muster the energy to offer an opinion on the situation. It took every scrap of power he had to concentrate, to keep from slipping over the edge into the black void of unconsciousness.

"I can handle this, Ms. Kincaid. I was a medic in 'Nam. It's not as serious as it looks."

"He'll need medication—"

"It'll be taken care of ma'am."

Shane forced his eyes open a slit and caught the look Alaina Montgomery shot at Del. "Lord, they're worse than the damn Boy Scouts—always prepared."

Suddenly Mr. Fitz loomed overhead like a giant billy goat, scratching at his snaggled whiskers, an unholy light in his eyes. The smell of fish hung around him like an acrid cloud. "Lord, ladies, what did ye do to the rascal? Did he have it comin'?"

"Mr. Fitz, please stand back," Matthews asked, exasperated. The towheaded agent leaned over Shane with a penlight, checking his pupils for response.

Shane squeezed his eyes shut. When he opened them again, Faith was bent over him, concern etched in every feature of her heart-shaped face. She sure was pretty, he noted, needing something to fasten his mind on. Her teeth dug into her full lower lip. He remembered how sweet that lip tasted—like cherry soda. She reached down and stroked his cheek with fingertips that felt like icicles on his burning skin.

She was worried about him. It was there in her lovely sable eyes, but Shane could feel it more than see it. He grasped it with a sense that had no name and wasn't counted among the five most normally used. He could feel Faith's concern. And he wondered, just before he lost consciousness, what it would be like to let down his guard and let this woman's concern touch his innermost self, the lonely man he kept locked inside him behind walls of wariness and cynicism.

Heaven. It would be like heaven, but heaven was a long way out of his reach.

The dream he fell into was an old one. For months it had been his nightly companion, but he had gradually banished it. In recent years it had returned to haunt him only when he had been too weak to fight it off. This was one of those times. The shiver that coursed through his big body as the scene began to unfold in his mind was one of dread. A sick sense of anticipation twisted like a knife in his chest.

Ellie Adamson. She stood at the end of a long, white corridor, nothing more than a dark silhouette at first. As he rushed toward her, her features became visible. She looked so young, with her pixie face and short fair hair.

Sweet, idealistic Ellie. She shouldn't have been

the one to stumble across the conspiracy at the training center in Quantico. Shane knew he should have been able to talk her out of involving herself in the case. He shouldn't have fallen in love with her. He shouldn't have let her die.

It was his fault. Ellie had stayed in because of him. She had died because of him. And his punishment was to watch it happen again and again in his dreams.

Always it happened in slow motion, increasing Shane's belief that he should have been able to prevent the tragedy. But he hadn't been able to move fast enough in reality, and he never could in his dreams either. Every time it was the same. He could see her turning toward him, see the light of recognition in her eyes, see her reach out to him, see the bullet explode into her chest.

As he held her and felt the life seep out of her, he brushed her hair back . . . and looked down on the face of Faith Kincaid.

"No!" he shouted.

It wouldn't happen again. He wouldn't let it happen again. Gathering what strength he had, he pushed Faith from his arms and the nightmare from his mind.

Promptly he fell into another dream. The Silvanus bust. He'd spent three years submerged in their organization. They were men who dealt daily in drugs and extortion, then went home at night to families. They talked about contracts on people's lives the same way ordinary businessmen talked about mergers and acquisitions. They were men who took the idea of the American dream and twisted it inside out until it was an ugly, surrealistic nightmare.

Shane had despised them for what they were. By the end of the case he had nearly come to despise himself. He had gotten too close, lost his focus, lost his edge, and nearly lost his life because of it. He could still see Adam Strauss's face twisted in rage, still hear the hoarse cry as the man realized Shane was the one who had betrayed him and the organization he worked for. Once again Shane felt the bullet slam into his shoulder.

The dream became even more disjointed then. There were bits and pieces of memory from the emergency room and the hospital. He listened again to John Banks's slow monotone explanation of Strauss's escape, and to reassurances spoken in the same emotionless tone of voice.

"He'll never find you, Shane. We covered your tracks so well, it looks like you vanished into thin air."

Then he saw himself floating through the black void of space, touching nothing and no one.

Faith dipped the washcloth into the pan of water again, wrung it out, and lifted it to Shane's forehead. He tried to push her away and twisted restlessly on the sheets. Dodging his arm, she shushed him and pressed the cool cloth to his brow.

Matthews had diagnosed the problem as an infection to the gunshot wound in Callan's shoulder. The necessary medications had magically appeared and been administered. He had assured Faith all they had to do now was wait for the drugs to kick in. Shane would be fine in a day or so. This wasn't anything he hadn't gone through before.

A gunshot wound. That ought to tell you something, Faith Kincaid, she thought with a sigh, as she sat back in her chair beside his bed. This was a man to steer clear of. He wasn't a part of the world in which she wanted to exist. She was an ordinary woman with ordinary needs and dreams.

At any rate she wasn't the sort of person who craved a lot of excitement. She didn't need to get involved with people who took getting shot in stride as a normal hazard of their everyday lives.

But when Shane moaned in his sleep, she bent over him to stroke a soothing hand along the hot, rough, beard-shadowed plane of his cheek. The action was as automatic as breathing. She responded to him on an instinctive level. Just as she had turned to him when she had been stricken with fear, she could not turn away from him while he was stricken with fever.

Fever wasn't all that was plaguing him, she thought, as she tried to quiet him. He moaned and mumbled protests, his head snapping from side to side on the pillow. Sweat beaded again on his forehead as he struggled with some hidden demon. Faith thought of the emotions she had heard in his music—the longing, the loneliness—and wondered if there was any connection to what haunted his dreams.

Romanticizing again, Faith, she scolded herself, and nibbled on her lip.

In all fairness it was difficult not to fantasize, considering the circumstances. She felt like the heroine of a historical novel, a damsel nursing a fallen knight—who happened to be more handsome than the devil himself. With a sigh she sat back and studied him as he settled into a deeper sleep.

Again the lines of his face struck her as being aristocratic—the high cheekbones, the straight nose, the finely chiseled mouth. Even in sleep it was a strong face. And the strength continued down the corded muscles of his neck to his broad shoulders. Whorls of black hair adorned the planes of his chest and swirled down in a line bisecting his abdomen, disappearing beneath the sheet he kept trying to kick off. Faith's cheeks bloomed fuchsia as her imagination rushed to picture the half of him covered by eyelet-edged ecru linen. If the top half of him was anything to go by, the bottom half of him had to be breathtaking.

Who was he, she wondered, trying frantically to get her mind off his anatomy. Where was he from?

What was his family background? How could she be so attracted to him without knowing these vital bits of information? She wasn't the sort to fall for a man based on looks alone.

Her gaze wandered around his room, taking in every detail that might give her some clue to the enigma that was Shane Callan. He was neat. His clothes hung in the armoire rather than over the furniture. What few personal items he left out were on the oak nightstand. There was a silver flask, a pack of cigarettes, two guns, and a book of poetry.

Smith and Wesson, and William Butler Yeats.

He was a riddle inside a puzzle inside an elegantly handsome facade.

Unable to stop herself, Faith reached out with one finger and traced the length of his arm. It was a trail that followed the hills and valleys of muscle of a man who used his body as well as his mind. The hair on the back of his forearm rasped gently against her fingertips, and tingles of awareness shot through her. She pulled her hand away as if his fevered skin had singed her. Her gaze jerked back up to his shoulder, where a fresh bandage covered the bullet wound that was giving him such grief.

She wanted a simple life, a quiet life.

"No, Faith," she whispered to herself. Even now attraction tugged between them, but she denied it. "You don't want to get involved with this man."

FIVE

"You look lots better."

Shane's brows shot up as he opened his eyes and slowly turned his head on the pillow to see little Lindy planted beside his bed, staring up at him with an expression of almost adult certainty on her cherubic face. Remnants of her bout with the chicken pox dotted her cheeks and forehead, but her dark eyes glowed with energy.

"Me and Mama are taking care of you," she informed him, lifting a small red plastic case onto the bed. Opening it, she revealed an array of miniature doctor's tools and a stash of candy. "It's my turn now 'cause Mama's busy. We have to see if you have a temp'ture. Open up!"

Obediently Shane opened his mouth and let Lindy stick a toy thermometer between his teeth. She pulled a pint-sized stethoscope out of her case, stuck the ends in her ears, and pressed the business end to his muscular biceps.

"Hmm..." she mused, pursing her lips, her eyebrows pulling together in thought.

"Well, nurse," he asked soberly, "what do you think?"

Lindy beamed a smile at him, dimples cutting into her rosy cheeks. "I think you're all better enough to color for a little while, but Mama will probably make you take a nap after that."

Pushing her doctor's bag aside, she scrambled up on the bed beside him with a coloring book and box of crayons clutched to her.

Keeping a discreet hold of the quilt that covered him, Shane eased himself up so he could lean back against the headboard. He tucked the blankets tightly around his waist, and Lindy settled in against his good side, as content and trusting as if she had known him her whole life.

A mysterious knot lodged itself in Shane's throat. He swallowed it down and told himself he was just thirsty. He wasn't in the least affected by this sweet, innocent darling with the unruly blond curls. Not in the least.

"This is the color book Aunt Jayne gave me for having the chicken spots," Lindy explained as she opened the book to a fresh page and offered Shane his pick of the crayons. "I'm sharing it with you because I think you're nice."

Oh, hell, Shane thought, selecting a stubby blue crayon, of course he was affected. He and little Lindy were from opposite ends of the spectrum. She was everything good, and he had seen everything evil, yet Faith's daughter cuddled against his side in her fuzzy pajamas, completely unconcerned. How could that irony not bring out all his protective instincts?

"Aunt 'Laina gave me that nurse game," Lindy explained as she started in enthusiastically on a picture of the Care Bears. "She said I could grow up to be a doctor, and she would chase the am'blances." She scrunched up her little pixie face and giggled. "Isn't that silly?"

Shane chuckled. He should have been hauling himself out of bed and seeing to the case, but somehow the idea didn't appeal to him as much as sharing these few moments with this child.

You're losing it, Callan, his little inner voice muttered. For once he managed to ignore it.

Faith froze in the doorway, then sagged against the jamb. Nothing had prepared her for the sight before her or for the effect it had on her heart. Shane, sitting up in bed, bare-chested, black hair tousled, looking impossibly masculine and sexy and in need of a shave. And Lindy curled up against his side in her pink pajamas, jabbering away a mile a minute as the pair of them colored.

"Lord, don't do this to me," Faith whispered despairingly. She was too exhausted, too emotionally drained right now to fight off the wave of feelings that assaulted her on seeing that big tough cop coloring with her four-year-old daughter. Wearily she closed her eyes.

In a flash every memory she had of Shane Callan passed through her mind—his initial arrogance, the intense sadness of his music, his vulnerability as he'd lain sick with fever and whatever memories tortured his sleep. She thought of the book of poetry she'd found on his nightstand. She thought of the incredible physical magnetism that drew her to him. Then she opened her eyes and looked at him again as he bent his dark head and murmured something that made Lindy giggle.

And in that instant Faith fell hopelessly, totally in love.

It wasn't a pleasant thing. It wasn't flowers and church bells and bird song. It was a long hard fall down a bumpy hill to the rocks of reality. She was in love with a man who distanced himself from people. He kept to himself behind a wall of cynicism and distrust. She didn't want to be in love with him. Any woman with an ounce of common sense would have taken one look and known Shane Callan was nothing but a heartbreaker.

That had to mean she didn't have a shred of intelligence then, because she was looking at him now, and all she wanted was to go join him on that bed and have him take her in his strong arms and hold her.

The fingers of her left hand curled around the smooth wood of the door frame as if to keep her from giving in to that desire. It seemed she didn't have the strength or the sense to keep from loving the wrong man. First William Gerrard, now Shane Callan.

"Darn it all," she muttered on a sigh of resignation. Why did she have to be such a blasted romantic? Bryan had always counseled her to hang on to that trait. He'd said the world needed more romantics. Maybe that was true, Faith thought, but why the heck did she have to be one of them?

"Hi, Mama!" Lindy chirped, shooting her a grin that was lacking a tooth on the upper right-hand side. "Me and Shane are coloring!"

Faith gathered herself together and stepped into the room, trying to look unruffled. "Lindy, sweetie, you shouldn't be in here. Mr. Callan needs his rest."

"But he's all better," Lindy said earnestly. Twisting around to look up at Shane, she said in a loud whisper, "Told you she'd make you take a nap."

"Scoot, pumpkin."

Lindy crumpled against her oversize playmate and sent her mother her most plaintive look. "Can't we color a little more? Please, Mama. Shane's real good. He stays inside the lines."

Shane lifted the book for her perusal, looking up

at her with smoky eyes as a lock of night black hair tumbled across his forehead. "See, Mom?"

His voice was low and rough, more so than usual. This was probably what he sounded like first thing in the morning or just after making love. Faith's skin blossomed with heat at the images that thought evoked.

"Very nice." She shot him a wry look and motioned her daughter toward the door. "Lindy, go on and see what Aunt Jayne is watching on TV."

Pouting, Lindy gathered her toys together and climbed down from the bed. A disgruntled frown marred her forehead as she grumbled, "All she ever watches is movies, and I fall asleep 'cause I'm too little."

Faith shook her head as she watched her daughter shuffle dejectedly out into the hall.

"I'll have to have a talk with her about wandering into people's rooms before the inn opens for business," she said. "That could be a very embarrassing habit for her to get into."

"Not to mention prematurely educational," Shane quipped, enjoying the color that rose in Faith's cheeks. He had to admit he found her modesty refreshing and sweet, and damned if it didn't turn him on. Desire stirred lazily inside him as he wondered whether or not she would be shy with him in bed.

"I'm sorry if she woke you."

"She didn't bother me at all," he said, a little surprised that it was true. It had been so long since he'd had the chance to be around small children, he'd forgotten how much he enjoyed their company. "Anyway, I have a feeling it's time I got up."

"You're in no condition to get up," Faith protested, planting her hands on her gently rounded hips and giving him a look of maternal command, even though maternal was the last thing she felt when she looked at him.

"That never stopped me before." He actually found the makings of a smile to send her. Unconsciousness had done wonders for his temperament.

If he had looked sexy before, Faith thought, he looked doubly so now, alone in the bed with the covers riding low on his flat belly. Darn it, why couldn't the government have sent her a fat, balding toad of a special agent?

Breathlessly she asked, "How are you feeling?"

"Fine." His brain felt like steel wool, his shoulder throbbed, and his skin hurt all over, but these complaints seemed minor enough to fit under the heading of "fine." By the look of her Faith wasn't able to make the same claim.

Shadows hung under her dark eyes in violet crescents. The pallor of her skin was a sharp contrast to the soft pink sweater she wore above a mauve cotton skirt that was gathered at the waist and hung down well past her knees. She was unquestionably as nervous as a cat and looked as if she had never even heard of a good night's sleep, let alone enjoyed one.

"How long have I been out?" Shane asked, scratching at the stubble that covered his lean cheeks.

"About nineteen hours," she answered as she flitted about his room like a hyperactive butterfly, straightening things that had already been straightened a dozen times and had never needed it in the first place. She could have told him how long he'd been out to the minute, but she didn't think it would be a wise thing to reveal, considering how it would reflect on her.

"Agent Matthews says the wound in your shoulder is infected." She started leaning in the direction of the door, eager to make her escape. "I should go get him. He'll want to see you."

Shane's right hand snaked out and closed quickly

but gently around her delicate wrist, snaring her alongside his bed. Her eyes rounded in alarm.

"That can wait," he said. "I want to talk to you first. What happened?"

"You passed out." Somehow Faith knew it wasn't the answer he was looking for, but it was the only one she wanted to give him.

He shook his head impatiently. "While I was out, what happened?"

She frowned at his suddenly wary look. "You didn't reveal any state secrets, if that's what you're worried about. You growled and snarled and were generally unpleasant, but that wasn't anything I hadn't already experienced."

"What else?" he prodded.

"Nothing, really."

She was a terrible liar. Her teeth dug into her lower lip, and her gaze darted around the room, landing everywhere but on him. She was keeping something from him. Even if it hadn't been written all over her lovely face, Shane could sense the tension in her.

Instead of wanting to shake the truth out of her, he found himself wanting to pull her into his arms and coax it out of her with gentle kisses. That was a bad idea, but he was darn near beyond caring about job ethics where Faith Kincaid was concerned. Just looking at her, even now when he was only at half strength, he wanted her. He was beginning to think they were simply going to have to deal with that desire sooner or later, because it obviously wasn't going to go away.

At the moment, though, his first concern had to be finding out what had happened while he'd been dead to the world.

"Faith?"

She trembled as his smoky voice caressed her like velvet. His thumb gently rubbed circles at the paper-thin flesh on the inside of her wrist. She felt faint from trying to fight her own emotions. Darn him anyway, what did he want to know? That she had sat beside him during the worst of his fever trying to comfort and soothe him? That she had just fallen in love with him because he had stayed inside the lines when he colored Bedtime Bear? That she was so stressed out, all she wanted to do was find a quiet place, curl into a ball, and cry?

"Did you get another call?"

"No," she said too quickly. "And Agent Matthews is handling everything, so you don't have to worry—"

Shane cut her off with a virulent expletive. "The bastard called again. Get me my pants."

Faith jerked her arm from his grasp and retreated two steps but faced him with a look of determination. "I will not get you your pants, Shane Callan. You are going to stay in bed at least another day."

"The hell I am."

Without warning or compunction he tossed back the covers and hauled himself to his feet, absolutely, magnificently naked.

Faith's jaw dropped. He was everything she had imagined he would be and then some. Six feet, four inches of beautifully sculpted, elegantly built man. Someone should have bronzed him and put him on display in a museum. His powerful chest tapered to gracefully slim hips that led to muscular thighs and impressive evidence of his gender.

"Sweetheart," he said in a voice like raw silk, "if you keep looking at me that way, neither one of us is going to need clothes in a minute."

As impossible as it seemed, Faith was certain she blushed an even deeper shade of red. The heat in her cheeks rose another million degrees. Arrogant, presumptuous man! Never mind that her insides were melting like ice cream under a hot July sun, he needn't have commented on it.

Quickly she turned and reached into the wardrobe. She yanked out one of the fresh bath towels she had stocked it with and thrust it at him.

"You are not leaving this room," she announced, refusing to look at him another second for fear that she'd faint dead away. It seemed all her bones had turned to butter.

"I'm here to take care of you," Shane pointed out, accepting the towel. "Not the other way around."

"It seemed a moot point when you were unconscious."

"I'm not unconscious anymore."

"So I noticed," Faith grumbled between her teeth, forcing her eyes to remain riveted to the pattern of the wallpaper.

"This is my case," Shane said as he slung the swath of deep green terry cloth around his hips and secured it out of deference to Faith's modesty. "I'm perfectly capable of handling it."

"Yes, I seem to remember you mumbling something to that effect as Mr. Matthews and Mr. Fitz hauled your semiconscious body from the floor of my room."

Shane ignored her sarcasm and abruptly went to the heart of the matter. "Was it the same caller? Did Matthews have time to trace it?"

"It was a letter, not a call," Faith admitted in a low voice. Lust was instantly forgotten. She trembled as she thought of the note that had come in the morning mail. It seemed impossible for a scrap of paper to be such a terrifying thing, but it had shaken her almost as badly as the phone call had. She didn't want Shane to know that, though. The pigheaded man belonged in bed. "Everything is under control. Your men are watching the house, and Agent Matthews is taking care—"

"What kind of letter?"

"A nasty one," she said, her voice soft and tight. "It was typed on plain notebook paper and stuck in a cheap envelope postmarked Fort Bragg. No fingerprints, according to Mr. Matthews."

"Damn," Shane muttered.

"My sentiments exactly."

She looked so fragile suddenly, so small and alone it tore at Shane. She stood there, looking away from him, staring at one of the wreaths of dried flowers that adorned the wall. Her arms were crossed tightly in front of her as if to keep her upright. The lady was putting on a hell of a show at being strong enough to handle this ugly business. Even as he cursed the man who was causing her trouble, he had to admire Faith's courage.

"You could back out on testifying, you know," he said softly, giving in to the need to offer her an option. Banks wouldn't have liked it, but Banks wasn't there watching this sweet flower tremble under the pressure. "It would hurt the case, but no one would blame you."

Faith shook her head. She would not back down. Especially not now. William Gerrard had manipulated her for too long. She had run across the country to escape him, and he was still trying to control her. She wasn't going to let him go on doing it.

"Everything's going to be fine," she said, almost to herself. "No one can actually get to me. Banks said so. You said so. Agent Matthews said so. Anyway, he's just trying to scare me."

And doing a damn good job of it, Shane thought. When he got his hands on the man responsible for terrifying her . . . In the meantime, he wanted to get his hands on Faith. The first time she had turned to him in fear, he had wanted to take her in his arms, but he had stopped himself. He didn't try to stop himself this time, nor did he question the wisdom of his decision. This was what she needed, and he was going to give it to her.

Gently he wrapped his good arm around her slender shoulders, frowning when she tensed at his touch. "You are scared," he said simply.

Her answer was little more than an exhalation of breath. "Yes."

"It's all right," he whispered, drawing her to his chest. When she gave in and leaned against him, he stroked his big hand over her soft tangle of fiery gold curls. "I'll take care of you."

Faith let her arms sneak around his lean waist. She let her cheek press against the warm flesh of his bare chest. She indulged herself for this one moment. It felt so good to be in his arms. She felt a sense not only of safety, but of rightness. Something deep inside her told her it was where she belonged. Whether that was true or not, it was where she wanted to be.

Shane was warm and real, an anchor in the

storm, her battered knight sworn to protect her. That was a romantic notion of a very unromantic situation, but Faith didn't care. She let her mind shut down and her senses take over. She thought of nothing but the way it felt to be held. She drank in the warm male scent of Shane. She listened to the strong, steady beat of his heart beneath her ear. Her fingertips memorized the marble-smooth planes of his back.

For a long moment they just stood there, bathed in the amber glow of the small hurricane lamp on the nightstand. Faith felt as if she were drawing strength from Shane, even though he had to have precious little to spare. The past few days had worn her down to nothing. Between dealing with threats and intrusions and Lindy's chicken pox and Shane's fever, she had depleted every milliliter of energy she had. But standing there with Shane's arm around her and her arms around him, she felt her power level rise.

"I'll be all right," she said, managing a smile as she looked up at him.

The impact of his gaze was like a physical blow that knocked the wind out of her lungs. His silver-gray eyes captured hers with a stare that was intense and predatory and possessive and so very basically male, everything feminine inside her responded. In that instant all the complications of their situation seemed to fall away, leaving just the two of them, just a man and a woman and a desire that was not to be denied.

Shane's mouth swooped down, trapping Faith's, taking hers in a kiss that was surprisingly tender, but barely tame. She let herself be swept along on the tide of passion as his tongue swept against hers. His fingers tangled in her hair as he tilted her head, giving him a better angle so he could deepen the kiss even more.

It was incredible how quickly and powerfully he could arouse the dormant woman inside her, Faith thought dimly, the woman her husband had never really wanted, the woman who had longed for love and passion. The needs of that woman caught fire like dry tinder touched to flame. Her body molded herself to his powerful frame, seeking total contact. Her breasts swelled against the steel of his chest. His good arm banded around her waist, lifting her and pulling her against his arousal.

Desperation and desire swirled together inside Faith like a whirlpool. She had waited a lifetime to feel what she was feeling now with Shane Callan, but once the danger had passed, he would be gone, and she would be left with a lifetime to wish she'd never laid eyes on him.

Shane was fighting his own inner battle. He knew to get too close to Faith Kincaid emotionally would be disastrous for both of them. Circumstances dictated that he offer her nothing but protection. Still, he had never known such a fierce desire to possess.

"I want you," he whispered against her lips, simplifying the problem to the lowest common denominator. The ache of his need was not going to lessen. Their circumstances were not going to change. The only solution was to draw a line—satisfy the physical desire, safe in the knowledge that neither would ask for anything more from the other.

Faith didn't have to hear the words to know what Shane was proposing. He wasn't the kind of man to make empty promises. He wasn't talking about love, but sex. For her there would be no separation of the two. As much as she wished she weren't, she was in love with him. She wanted him, but she wanted his heart as well as his body. And while he stood nearly naked in the circle of her arms, more than ready to make good on his claim, she knew his body was all he was willing to give her.

"I don't know if I can deal with this," she said, deciding to take the coward's way out for the moment. She stepped out of his embrace, immediately feeling cold and alone. "You should go back to bed. You need your rest."

"That's not my only need. What about you, Faith? A woman has needs too."

How true, she thought. She had physical needs, needs that had long been neglected, needs that seemed to double and triple when she was in the same room with him. At this very moment her whole body was throbbing with the need he aroused in her. Her breasts swelled for his touch. The feminine core of her ached with an emptiness she wanted only Shane to fill. But her needs went beyond the physical, and his offer didn't.

Shane sighed and raked a hand back through his tousled hair. "I won't lie to you, Faith. I want a physical relationship with you, but I can't give you anything more. That may sound callous, but it's necessary. I think it's best to be honest up front."

She wanted to call him a liar despite what he'd said. He wouldn't want her to be honest. He wouldn't want to hear she was in love with him. Faith knew that as sure as she knew her own name. Shane was a man who shunned emotional entanglements. Even in his sleep he had tried to push her away. The man needed love, but she was certain he wouldn't want it if she offered it to him on a platter.

"I have to put Lindy to bed," she said, turning away from him, exhaustion weighing down on her like a huge stone.

Shane nodded, letting her walk away even though his body was aching for release. If she felt half the attraction he did, she wouldn't be able to deny it for long. If nothing else, she would end up using it as an excuse to escape her other problems for a few brief hours. And that would be just as well, he thought, for all concerned. That kind of escape was the only thing he had to offer her. "I'll be here when you change your mind."

Faith paused at the door, almost smiling at his choice of words. She didn't look back at him as her heart asked the question she didn't dare voice— *You'll be here when I change my mind, but will you be here afterward?*

SIX

"WE'RE ONE STEP closer," Shane said into the phone, wishing he had more to report to his boss. He took a long drag on his cigarette and leaned back in the squeaky desk chair, his gaze idly wandering around Faith's little office. "The letters have all been postmarked in nearby towns. The call we managed to trace came from a phone booth in Ukiah. We know he's in the immediate area."

"The sixty-four-thousand-dollar question is: Where?" Banks asked in his typical sardonic tone.

"I don't know," Shane admitted, narrowing his eyes as he stared at the neatly typed, utterly nasty missive lying on the walnut desk before him. It was the third Faith had received in a week. Tension coiled in his gut. He didn't like playing a waiting game. He was a hunter by nature. But in this scenario he was relegated to the role of fisherman—waiting for their boy to take the bait so he could reel him in.

"How's our witness holding up?"

Shane thought of Faith. She had an inner strength that never failed to amaze him. The constant tension was taking a toll on her, but every time he expected her to give in or give up she reached deep down inside for a little more grit. "She's a remarkable lady."

"Yes, she is. Give her my regards...and my condolences for having to put up with you day in and day out."

A wry smile quirked up one corner of Shane's mouth as he tossed out a rather lewd suggestion about what his superior could do with the rest of his day.

"Hang tight, pal," Banks advised, chuckling at Callan's characteristic disregard for authority figures. "Gerrard's request for a later court date has been denied. He'll be sweating bullets soon if he doesn't hear word of Faith backing out on testifying. They'll make a move soon."

"I'll be here when they do," Shane promised. He could almost taste the vengeance. Damn, that wasn't like him. An agent couldn't take cases personally and hold together for long. Pushing the thought from his mind, he changed the subject. "Any word on Strauss?"

"Interpol says he was spotted in Argentina."

"I don't think so," Shane said slowly, that knot of tension tightening in his belly as he called to mind the image of his archnemesis from the Silvanus organization. During his three years on the case he had come to know the man as well as he knew himself. Adam Strauss may have had Argentina in mind as a new base of operations, but Shane knew with a cold certainty he wouldn't be there yet. "That's not his style."

"Meaning he'd kill you first before retiring to a tropical paradise?"

"He swore he would. As incongruous as it sounds, Adam Strauss is a man of his word."

"Can't happen, my friend. There's no way he can find you."

After Shane ended the conversation and hung

up the phone, he sat back. Where there's a will, there's a way, he thought with an odd kind of detachment. But Adam Strauss wasn't his immediate concern.

Stubbing out his cigarette, he forced his mind back to the matter at hand. His gaze devoured the letter Faith had received the day before. There simply wasn't anything about it that pointed in any one direction. The only thing they could discern from it was that the perpetrator had a violent imagination and a solid command of grammar.

"Damn," he muttered, shaking another cigarette out of the rapidly depleting pack. He dangled it from his lip and momentarily forgot about it.

He was getting itchy. Patience was the name of the game on a case like this one, but his was wearing thin around the edges. He wanted a suspect, and they didn't have one. He didn't like Faith's caretaker, Mr. Fitz, but so far the only thing he could accuse the man of was being ill-tempered and malodorous.

Maybe, Shane mused, the real reason he was getting edgy was because there was something he wanted more than a suspect—Faith. Nearly a week had passed since their encounter in his bedroom.

She hadn't taken him up on his offer of a physical relationship, but that wasn't because she wasn't interested. It was obvious she was very aware of him as a man. She was skittish around him, a kind of nervousness that sprang from sexual tension.

Lying in bed every night, knowing she was just across the hall, was an experience Shane considered on a level with Chinese water torture. He couldn't remember ever wanting a woman the way he wanted her. He was a relatively young, healthy male with strong sexual appetites, but this transcended mere physical need. Want of her seemed to have invaded every level of his being. The idea made him uncomfortable, but he couldn't escape it. If he didn't get her into bed soon and slake this need, it was going to drive him right over the edge.

All he had to do was push her a little. Faith was too inexperienced to resist a skilled seduction. But he couldn't do that and live with himself afterward. As unappealing as the idea was, he was just going to have to bide his time.

"Good Lord!" Faith choked as she opened the door. Blinking rapidly as she entered the office, she waved an arm in front of her as if she were cutting her way through a jungle with a machete. "What are you trying to do, give yourself lung cancer in one sitting?"

Shane frowned but couldn't quite stop himself from snatching the unlit cigarette from his lip. Faith's voice had that innate motherly quality that could make even a grown man feel contrite. "We'll have the place fumigated for you after we leave."

Faith almost flinched at the words. After he left. The thought caused an alarming amount of pain. Forcing herself past the sensation, she said, "Alaina and Jayne are both gone for the day. I gave them time off for good behavior above and beyond the call of duty. I'm going to take Lindy down to the beach for the afternoon. I thought you'd want to know."

"Fine." Shane pushed himself to his feet with the lazy, deceptive grace of a big cat. "I'll go with you."

It was on the tip of her tongue to say no, but Faith bit the automatic response back. In the first place it wouldn't do any good. Mules had nothing on Shane Callan when it came to being stubborn. In the second place, it wasn't what she really wanted. The thought of spending the day on the beach with him held the appeal of forbidden fruit. It may not have been wise, but she allowed herself to yield to the temptation.

"All right. We'll be ready as soon as I pack the picnic basket."

Beauty was something Shane had had little room for in his life in recent years. Now it surrounded him. He felt it wash over him like the golden sunlight pouring down out of the clear blue sky. He could feel it warming him and healing him—not just the wound in his shoulder, but the scars that lacerated his soul as well. He could feel it seeping inside him and filling up all the dark corners.

Beauty was the fresh, cool salt air, the temporary absence of tension, Lindy's laughter as bubbling little waves chased her up the beach.

Natural beauty was obvious all around. They had set up their little picnic site on a secluded strip of soft, silvery sand. Shane lay stretched out on a blue plaid blanket, propped up on his right elbow, his gaze automatically sweeping the area. A hundred feet or so above them, at the top of a rugged cliff, stood the inn, its assortment of roof peaks zigzagging across the azure sky. Before them stretched the

Pacific, shining like a jewel in the setting of a perfect day. Fishing boats dotted the far horizon, and gulls swooped and called overhead.

Also coming under the heading of natural beauty was Faith. She walked along the water's edge, helping her daughter hunt for seashells. Somewhere during the last week Shane had lost his mental image of her as William Gerrard's wife, the polished society lady. That wasn't Faith. Faith was scrubbed-fresh skin and unruly curls, faded jeans and canvas sneakers. She was a sweet smile and an intricately wrought golden heart. She was beauty—outwardly and inwardly.

Her kind of beauty was something a man could grow used to in a hurry and live with a long time.

"What are you thinking?" Faith asked with a guileless smile as she plopped down on the blanket to sit cross-legged beside him.

Through the dark lenses of his sunglasses Shane studied her for a moment before answering. She shoved up the sleeves of her baggy navy sweatshirt and snagged back a handful of wind-tossed hair. The sun had raised soft color in her cheeks and teased out a smattering of freckles on her nose.

"That you're beautiful," he said simply, his statement carrying almost none of the emotion that was struggling to come to life inside him.

Faith was stunned to absolute silence. Her heart did a swan dive into her stomach. The last thing she had expected from a man like Shane was pretty words. For a long moment she sat staring at him like a doe caught in the headlights of an oncoming truck.

Even in this setting he looked tough and dangerous. He had donned jeans and a black sweatshirt for their outing, leaving his shoulder holster behind, but not his pistol. The gun had been his contribution to the picnic basket.

A man who packed guns in picnic baskets had told her she was beautiful, had stated it as if it were a plain, irrefutable fact. A smart woman wouldn't have gone marshmallow soft inside over that. Faith decided her brain shouldn't enter into the debate. It didn't seem to function well at all when it came to this man.

A frown tugged at the corners of Shane's mouth. "You act as if you've never had a man tell you that."

"I haven't," she admitted. "Not someone who really meant it."

"Then your ex-husband is blind as well as stupid."

She sighed as she absently drew patterns in the sand with her finger. "Disinterested is probably the more accurate word."

"A fool."

"Let's not talk about him, okay?" she said, flashing Shane a brittle smile. "Let's just enjoy this beautiful day."

She brought her knees up and wrapped her arms around them. Turning her face to the sun, she closed her eyes and concentrated on absorbing the warmth. The whole point of coming to the beach had been to get away from her problems. Shane himself was a reminder, but Faith had decided simply to pretend he wasn't a government agent. For this afternoon he was just a man, they were just ordinary people enjoying the beach and the sun.

She didn't have time to do more than register the shadow that suddenly blocked the warm rays from her face. Before she could even open her eyes to see what was happening, Shane's mouth had settled against hers, and she was enveloped by warmth of another kind.

This was an inner heat that blazed whenever he

touched her. Faith let it sweep through her. She didn't try to fight the feelings that engulfed her. She'd been fighting them for too long. For this one kiss logic and reality could just butt out. She'd had enough reality to last her. This was escape, a wonderful fantasy, and she welcomed it.

Instinctively her hands came up to steady herself. She wound her arms around Shane's neck as he parted her willing lips and deepened the kiss. Masterfully he explored her mouth, tasting and claiming territory that had lain fallow for too long. Desire awakened inside her and came to life like a seed in the spring.

Slowly he eased her down to the blanket, never breaking the kiss. His left hand stole under the hem of her sweatshirt, and his fingers teased the silky flesh of her belly. She sucked in a breath as he dragged his lips across her cheek and jaw and slid his hand up to claim one aching breast.

"Shane," she managed to whisper, forcing her eyes open. "What are you doing?"

His eyes were the color of storm clouds when he lifted his head and looked down at her. He rubbed his thumb over the pebble-hard nub of her nipple and smiled with satisfaction as she gasped. His voice was like warm silk when he spoke. "I'm enjoying this beautiful afternoon."

A perfectly reasonable answer, Faith thought as her eyes drifted shut and her concentration focused on the incredible sensation of his hand on her breast. His long, elegant musician's fingers stroked and kneaded the soft globe of flesh. His thumb continually massaged the sensitive center. Tingling waves of sensation radiated from that point, shooting directly to the pit of her belly where they swirled in an ever tightening whirlpool.

Lord, she'd never known a man's touch could incite her senses to riot. This was incredible. This was something she had never experienced. She suddenly felt cheated. She'd been a wife and had never known this kind of physical pleasure. She was a grown woman with a child. . . .

"Lindy—" she said, abruptly trying to sit up and finding it a futile task with Shane half-sprawled on top of her.

"She can't see us." He raised up just enough to peer over the wicker food hamper that shielded their activities from Lindy's view. Faith's daughter sat playing in the sand a good thirty feet away. "She's completely absorbed in counting her seashells."

"That won't take long," Faith said on a breathless laugh. "She can only make it to ten."

"Lindy!" Shane called.

"I'm real busy!" she called back, not even lifting her head from her task.

"Okay. You give a holler when you're not busy anymore."

"Okie-dokie!"

Shane turned his attention from daughter to mother. Faith's heart-shaped face was flushed, her lips were love-swollen and glistened from his kiss. Possessive desire pounded through him in waves.

"I don't think this is a very good idea," Faith said weakly, thrills rippling through her at the hungry look on his face.

"Really?" One black brow quirked upward as Shane began to lower his head. "Then you're going to hate this."

He kissed her again, slowly, deeply, as if they had years for just this one kiss. Faith wished they did. She wished they had forever. Surely the love she'd stored up in her heart would last that long and then some. But they didn't have forever. They had only the present. Shane would be with her only a few weeks at the most.

Would the heartache be any less when he left if she said no to a physical relationship with him? Or would it be even more painful with the addition of regret for not taking as much as he was willing to give her?

Shane felt his heart twist when he raised his head and looked down into sable eyes swimming with tears of confusion. He cursed himself for complicating her already complicated situation. He had no business wanting Faith Kincaid in the first place. What the hell did he think he was doing pushing her this way? Not more than a few hours ago he'd told himself he wouldn't pressure her into anything.

Gently he brushed a crystal drop of moisture from the corner of her eye with his thumb. "No tears," he whispered, his expression more tender than he would have believed possible. "Today is too perfect for tears."

He was right, Faith thought, her heart aching with love for him as she traced her fingertips over the angular planes of his aristocratic face. There would be time enough for tears later.

"I want you, Faith," he said, his smoky voice a

caress to her already-aroused senses. "But I won't push you. It has to be your choice."

Lindy's voice floated to them on the breeze. "I'm all done being busy now!"

A rare smile lit Shane's face as he sat up and put his sunglasses back on. "I think that's our call to duty."

"Duty?" Faith questioned, slowly gathering her scattered wits. She took Shane's hand and let him help her up from the blanket.

"Construction crew. I promised Lindy I'd help her build a sand castle."

"You're a talented man, Mr. Callan."

He slid an arm around her shoulders as they headed up the beach. "I told you before, I'm full of surprises."

Faith leaned against him, silent, wondering if she dared hope one of the surprises inside him would be love.

He watched from the deck of the cabin cruiser, one eye pressed to the eyepiece of a state-of-the-art telescope. His blood heated as he watched them kiss and embrace. "Ah, yes," he murmured, "love is a many-splendored thing."

Sitting back in the comfortable helm seat on the navigation bridge, he propped his legs up on the railing and lazily polished the dull blue barrel of a semiautomatic pistol. "Love and death. How poetic. Soon Mrs. Gerrard, Agent Callan. Soon."

SEVEN

ONE SAND CASTLE turned into two and eventually became a minor megalopolis on the little beach. After the construction boom came a well-deserved cookie break, then Lindy curled up on the blanket with her bedraggled doll tucked to her chest and fell into the deep, blissful sleep of a happy child.

Faith gazed down on her daughter, gently rubbing a hand back and forth over Lindy's back as she slept. Shane watched quietly, his expression pensive as feelings tumbled loose inside him. He couldn't remember the last time he'd felt such a sense of peace. There was no denying that the source of that peace was the lady sitting across from him, and the little girl with the sun-blushed cheeks and yellow Big Bird sweatshirt.

"She's pretty special, isn't she?" he murmured, reaching out hesitantly to touch Lindy's silky hair. A curl wound around his finger.

Faith shot him a grin. "I hope you're not expecting an unbiased opinion. Personally I think the sun rises and sets on this little one."

"I've got a slew of nieces and nephews," Shane announced, almost as startled as Faith was that he had revealed something personal. Suddenly uneasy, he looked out at the ocean where fishing boats bobbed on the horizon. "I haven't seen them in a long time."

"Because of your job?"

"The life I lead is not conducive to emotional complications."

Faith didn't attempt to hold back her harsh laugh. "How clinically put."

"It's the truth." His answer was almost as sharp as the look he leveled at her. "Would you rather I lie to you, Faith?"

"No," she whispered. "I've been lied to enough."

Shane bit back an oath. He wasn't accustomed to explaining himself to anyone—quite the opposite, in fact—but one look at Faith's expression compelled him to tell her more. "If an agent lets emotions get in his way, he can screw things up. A clear head can mean the difference between life and death."

"So you just turn it off like a faucet?" she asked. That kind of control was well beyond her. She both envied and pitied him for it.

Shane let the question hang in the air. He didn't want to think about it today. Today the sun was shining on him. Today he could be with Faith and her daughter. He could pretend to be a normal man for a few hours. The shadows would swallow him up again soon enough.

Faith didn't press for an answer. She had more questions to ask, but she didn't voice any of them. Wasn't it a lonely way of life? She knew it was, she'd sensed the loneliness in him, she'd heard it in his music. Had he ever thought of quitting? That question was too dangerous. "No" would have been too painful an answer to hear.

"When I was a kid," he said, staring out at the

sea again, "my family had this place on the coast of Maine. We used to spend the whole summer there at the ocean."

Relieved that the sudden tension between them had evaporated, Faith soaked up the information he offered. She felt a little like a squirrel hoarding nuts in preparation for a long, bleak winter, secreting away what tidbits she could about this man. He liked poetry and music and children and summers by the sea. There was a side of him that wasn't dangerous at all. There was a side of him that was just a man, a man full of memories and loneliness, a man who needed love.

A week ago she had wondered if she had the strength to keep from loving him. Now her perspective was changing, and she began to wonder if she had the strength to give him her love. Could she offer the bounty of her heart, knowing he needed it but might not take it? Could she risk that kind of rejection again? Did she really have a choice?

They put off going back to the inn for as long as they could, trying to squeeze the most out of their golden afternoon. But as the fog bank began to drift in, they surrendered and gathered their things together.

The walk was made in near silence, with Lindy the only one in the mood for conversation. Shane was reticent by nature, but Faith thought she could sense another reason for his silence as they climbed the wooden stairs that zigzagged up the cliff from the beach—sadness.

For once she didn't scold herself for romanticizing. They had shared something very special. She was certain Shane was as reluctant to leave it behind as she was.

Faith watched him as he carried her daughter across the lawn toward the sprawling house, his head bent, expression serious as he listened attentively to Lindy's plans for the shells she had gathered. He was so patient and gentle with Lindy. William had offered his attention to his daughter only when there had been a press camera trained on him.

Stopping in her tracks, Faith hugged the folded blanket to her as she came to a decision. She loved Shane Callan. It didn't matter why. It didn't matter that he believed he could promise her nothing. She loved him, and she would take what time they had together to give him that love. If a future came of it, she would embrace that future wholeheartedly.

If nothing came of it, she would embrace the memories and harbor no regrets.

Shane stood beside his bed frowning as he slipped off his watch and put it on the nightstand. Sleep was going to be a long time coming tonight. Restlessness stirred within him. The day that had healed him with peace and sunlight was a memory now, and somehow that left him feeling unsettled.

Damn, he thought as he pulled his shirt off, he was getting melancholy in his old age. He was supposed to be thinking about surveillance and suspects, but his mind wanted to linger on thoughts of the beach and Lindy ... and Faith. Faith the woman, not the witness.

A soft knock drew his attention to the door.

"Shane?"

Her voice was soft and tentative, yet it seemed to reach through the door to caress him. His skin heated instantly at the thought. Before his hormones could run amuck, he called out, "Come in."

Faith slipped into the room like a thief, closing the door quietly behind her. When she turned to face him, Shane felt as though he'd taken a punch to the solar plexus. Faith stood there, her doe eyes wide and uncertain, the amber glow of the lamp teasing out the red lights in her hair. She wore an ivory satin robe that was belted at the waist and fell to the floor. Framed by the V neckline of her robe was the necklace she always wore. The delicate bit of gold glittered warmly above her heart.

"You said you'd be here when I changed my mind," she said, her gaze holding him captive. Her teeth grazed her lower lip, further betraying her nervousness. She swallowed and her breasts gave a little jump as she sucked in a breath. "I've changed my mind."

Shane held himself utterly still, as if he were afraid she would vanish if he moved. A heavy warmth surged through his body, settling in his groin. "Are you sure?"

Faith nodded, her heart in her throat. He had to be the sexiest thing on two legs, standing there beside the bed wearing nothing but his jeans. The look he leveled at her from under his straight black brows was fiercely intense, searching for any hint of uncertainty in her. "I'm sure."

Stepping away from the door, she closed the distance between them. Shane felt the level of his desire for her rise with every step she took. He wanted her. There was no need to question that, but he had to know she had no delusions about what this would mean. For both their sakes he couldn't afford to let it be anything more than a few sweet hours of bliss.

When she was standing no more than a caress away, he lifted a hand and tenderly brushed his knuckles against her cheek. "I can't make promises. You know that."

"I'm not asking for any," she whispered, her eyes downcast so he couldn't see that, while she wasn't asking him for promises, she was praying for a miracle. She would take whatever he would give her, but her heart was hoping that would be a lifetime.

Shane tipped her chin up, but before he could comment on what he saw in her gaze, she said, "I'd like to know what it is to have a man want me."

It was the truth. Sex with William had been infrequent and unsatisfying. Her ex-husband had never set her on fire with a look or a touch. He had viewed their physical relationship as a necessary evil, and she had accepted that with a mix of guilt and relief. It was Shane who had awakened the latent sensuality in her. It was Shane who made her feel like a woman, who made her yearn for a man's touch—for *his* touch.

Now he bent his head to hers, his gray eyes glowing with desire. "Lord, Faith," he said on a growl, "how could any man look at you and not want you?"

He kissed her with barely restrained passion, groaning as she melted willingly against him. With trembling hands he pushed the ivory robe back off her shoulders, exposing her bare skin to his touch. Satin whispered to the floor at their feet, and she was naked in his arms.

His lips trailed along her jaw to her throat as his fingers trailed down her supple back, and lower, to the full curve of her buttocks. He lifted her, fitting her against the erection that swelled and strained against the front of his jeans, letting her know just how much he wanted her.

Faith shuddered with raw anticipation. She gasped at the feel of him pressing intimately against her, and at the feel of her nipples burrowing into his chest hair. Need ribboned through her, brushing every nerve ending to awareness so that when Shane stood her away from his body, she nearly cried out at the sudden deprivation.

Mesmerized, she stared at him, her eyes passion-glazed and heavy-lidded as she watched him slowly lower the zipper of his jeans. Her breath held fast in her lungs as he peeled the denim from his lean hips and let the pants drop to join her robe on the floor. This wasn't the first time she had seen him naked, but the sight still sapped the strength from her knees. He was beautiful and completely unselfconscious as she feasted her eyes on him.

Time ticked by unheeded. Shane's gaze roamed as hungrily over Faith's body as hers did over his. She was utterly feminine, all soft curves and creamy flesh. Her breasts were full, their swollen mauve tips begging for his attention. Her small waist flared into womanly hips. The delta of soft curls at the juncture of her thighs was more red than gold, and Shane's whole body throbbed with the need to discover the sweet secrets that lay beyond.

Ruthlessly checking his own rampant desire, he reached out and took her hand. If passion was all he could give her, then he would make it as perfect for her as he knew how.

"It's been a long time for me," she said shyly.

Shane drew her into his arms and kissed her

tenderly. "Don't worry, honey. I'll take care of you. Just lie back and let me love you."

As they sank to the bed, Faith breathed in the mingled scents of potpourri and man. Shane slid down her body, his hands tracing every line and curve of her. He caressed her breasts, his fingers stroking and kneading. Gently he fastened his lips around one nipple and sucked at the eager peak. She moaned and writhed beneath him. Her back arched off the bed, pressing her breast even deeper into the heat of his mouth.

Shane swept one hand down her side and across her hip. His fingers slid through the downy curls that covered her femininity and delved between her parted thighs to stroke the essence of her. She responded with tight little whimpers that spurred him on. His own need was a savage ache in his groin, but his focus was on Faith. Her body was begging for release. He could sense how close to the edge she was, and he coaxed her closer still with his hand and mouth.

"No!" she whimpered, tears of disappointment sliding from the outer corners of her eyes as her pleasure crested abruptly in a blinding flash.

Shane was beside her in an instant to kiss the

moisture from her temples. "Shhh, honey, don't cry. What's wrong? Did I hurt you?"

"I wanted you...with me."

"I will be," he promised, nuzzling her cheek.

"You don't understand," Faith mumbled, feeling miserable and inadequate. "That won't happen for me again, Shane. I—"

"You don't think so?" he asked, smoothing a hand back through her tousled hair. His smile was uncharacteristically soft. "That was your first trip to heaven, sweetheart, but I promise you it won't be the last time I take you there tonight."

He couldn't promise her much, but that was one pledge he would definitely keep. He was a long way from being finished making love to this lady. His hunger for her was beyond anything he'd ever known. It was a hunger not only to take pleasure but to give it as well.

In the soft glow of lamplight be bathed her with kisses, his lips lingering over every detail of her face, her throat, her shoulders. He drank in the taste of her and the powder-soft rose-petal scent of her, absorbing every detail of her body, every nuance of her response.

Obediently passive beneath his tender assault,

Faith discovered she had erogenous zones she had never dreamed of. Shane's tongue flicking across the inner crease of her elbow made her gasp. A kiss planted on the back of her knee stopped her breathing altogether. And when he parted her thighs and settled his mouth against the most feminine part of her, she thought she would die of the pleasure.

Her first impulse was to push him away, but that response was quickly overruled by need, the need to have him touch her and love her and cherish her in every way he wanted. So she opened herself to his intimate kiss and this time when completion rushed through her, stunning her with shock wave after shock wave, she let herself be swept along on the tide. This time when he came back to her, she greeted him with a smile instead of tears.

"Can I touch you?" she asked softly.

Shane's eyes darkened from smoke to midnight at her request. He brought her hand up to his chest and abandoned it. "Please do."

Lovingly Faith stroked her fingertips over his chest, carefully avoiding the bandage on his left shoulder. Feeling wonderfully bold and uninhibited, she leaned over him and flicked her tongue across his flat brown nipple, then sent him a smile that was pure wickedness when he sucked in his breath. Her hand strayed down over his taut belly, following the line of downy black hair that ended in a thicket on his groin.

Gently she closed her hand around his arousal. Her groan of appreciation echoed Shane's. He was warm and hard, steel sheathed in velvet, throbbing with need for her ... as she was for him.

She turned to him with a look of near desperation and breathed his name. Shane needed no more invitation than that. He rolled Faith beneath him and kneeled between her thighs as he took care of protection. An instant later he was sinking into her embrace—the embrace of her arms and the embrace of her womanhood. Lifting her hips into his, she accepted him gradually, her tight warmth closing around him, welcoming him. He closed his eyes for a moment savoring the sensation of sweet bliss.

He loved her tenderly, gently, with slow, deep strokes that seemed to reach to the very heart of her. Faith held him, moved with him, letting her love for him pour out of her every way she could without actually speaking the words. She let her body tell him with each caress, with each sigh. And this time, when the end came for them both, the tears that filled her eyes were tears of love.

Shane turned onto his back and settled Faith against his side with her head pillowed on his good shoulder. He was exhausted, spent, which was to be expected, but there were other feelings he hadn't expected. Rightness, comfort, and a fullness in his chest he refused to name.

He had sought physical release in Faith's arms. He had told himself this would be only to ease the restless ache in his gut and to give Faith a few hours of escape from her worries. He hadn't expected the sweetness, the warmth this completion had brought. In giving him her body, Faith had given him much more. In her arms he had felt peace and tenderness and understanding.

For one unguarded moment he let himself wonder what it would be like to take what she offered— a haven, salvation, a place to rest and heal a world-weary heart. The thought of it was so beautiful, so tempting, it was frightening.

"I never knew," Faith whispered, her breath warm against his cooling skin. "In twelve years of marriage, I never knew anything like this."

Silently Shane cursed the bastard who had married

this gentle, giving woman only to further his career. William Gerrard deserved to be imprisoned for that alone.

His hand came up to stroke her hair possessively. "Why did you stay with him?" he asked, fighting to keep the harsh edge from his voice. "Did you love him?"

"At first," she said with a sad smile. "William can be very charming when it suits him. He swept me off my feet. Then, after he won his Senate seat and we moved to Washington, his interest in me waned. I blamed his job. I blamed myself. Eventually I got around to blaming William, but I made the mistake of believing he could change, that I could change him. I couldn't."

"Twelve years is a long time to spend trying to change somebody."

"Oh, I'd given up hope on him long before that."

"Then why did you stay with the bastard?" At one time he might have suspected her of marrying Gerrard for his money or for the glamour or power, but no such suspicions surfaced now. He had come to trust Faith as he trusted very few people.

"Because I'd taken a vow," she said, feeling both foolish and defensive. "I'd pledged to be his wife for better or worse. I believe in those vows. I know that sounds old-fashioned, but I do."

Shane wrapped his arms around her and pressed a kiss to her forehead. The cynic in him labeled her naive, but if she had been naive, she was also good and honest and sincere. Those were qualities he'd seen precious little of in the last few years. It made him feel old and jaded now to lie there with this treasure of a woman in his arms. He didn't deserve the chance to touch her, but damned if he could stay away from her.

The only thing he could offer her was protection from the man who had so callously used her. And that Shane pledged to her and to himself. "He'll never hurt you again, Faith. I'll see to it."

EIGHT

FAITH STUDIED SHANE'S face in the soft light of predawn. He frowned even in his sleep. She reached out and gently rubbed at the line between his dark eyebrows with the pad of her thumb, and a wave of love swept through her as he grumbled and tried to snuggle closer.

He'd been such a tender lover. Insatiable but tender, and considerate of their difference in size and of her lack of experience. She imagined Shane had been called many things in his time, and tender was probably not at the head of the list; but he had been tender with her, and she loved him for it.

Carefully, skillfully he had shown her fulfillment as she had never known it. He'd coaxed her away from inhibitions and uncertainties. He'd made her acutely aware of her femininity and her potential for sensuality. As they had made love, the cynical man had faded away, leaving a man she wanted to give her heart to, a sensitive man with musician's hands and the soul of a poet.

When he opened his eyes and looked across the pillow at her, Faith knew she had to tell him. It might have been safer to say nothing. Shane would no doubt have preferred she say nothing. But she couldn't keep this love to herself. Her heart was overflowing with it. There was every chance he wouldn't accept it, but Faith knew she had to offer it to him nevertheless.

"I want to tell you something," she whispered, lifting her hand to touch his beard-roughened cheek.

Shane turned his head and pressed a kiss to her palm. "What?"

"I love you."

Nothing had prepared Shane for the feelings that rushed through him at those words. The power of it was stunning... and terrifying. He raised up on one elbow and looked down at Faith, his ready argument against emotional entanglement sticking in his throat like a tennis ball.

Lord, she was so pretty, so sweet, and everything that was in her heart was in her eyes as well.

Longing surged within him to battle with logic. He couldn't let this happen. He had drawn the line, set the rules of their relationship for a reason. They couldn't step across that line. It wasn't safe.

"Faith, no—"

She silenced his denial with two slender fingers pressed to his lips. "I know it's not something you wanted to hear, Shane. I don't expect you to respond in kind. But you said you wanted us to be honest about our feelings up front, so that's what I'm doing."

"Faith, I—we—damn." He bit back a sigh. This was certainly proving his point. His emotions were short-circuiting his brain. All he wanted to do was look down at her. She was so lovely, so fragile, like something made of fine porcelain. He touched her cheek as if to assure himself she was indeed real. Then his fingers trailed down to her throat to brush across the gold heart she wore. When he spoke again, he chose his words carefully. The last thing he wanted was to hurt her. "Honey, you're in a high-stress situation. I'm here to protect you. We're attracted to each other. What you're feeling—"

"Is love," Faith said, heading him off at the pass.

"It's—"

"Love," she insisted, her delicate brows lowering over her eyes. The hardheaded man. He may not have appreciated the sentiment, but she wasn't about to let him talk her out of it either. "I know what's in my own heart, Shane. I can't say I was very happy about it when I first figured it out, but I can't deny it either. I love you whether we like it or not."

A ghost of a smile turned up the corners of Faith's lips as she took in Shane's dark expression. She'd been right in thinking he wouldn't want the love she offered, the love he needed, the love she needed to give. Being right was small consolation, but the struggle he seemed to be waging within himself gave life to a spark of hope. Maybe, if they could just have a little time together, maybe...

Maybe what, Faith, she asked herself. Maybe Shane would change, the way she had believed

William would change? Maybe they could live happily ever after? Maybe she was being a fool.

"I have to go back to my room," she whispered as tears filled her eyes. She blinked them back determinedly. "Lindy will be getting up soon. I just wanted you to know how I feel. We can have a few weeks together; I'll take whatever you're willing to give me. But if you decide you want more, we can have more."

We can have forever, she added silently.

She started to turn away from him to slide out of bed, but Shane's big hand on her shoulder stopped her. Without saying a word, he bent down and settled his mouth against hers in a hot, deep kiss, a kiss of raw, primitive possession. He swept a hand down her side to her hip to steady her as he kneed her thighs apart and eased into her with one slow thrust. Faith moaned at the feel of him filling her. Automatically her hips lifted to make his entrance easier.

"This is what I can give you, Faith," he murmured darkly against her lips as his body moved against her and within her, seeking the mind-numbing solace he found only with her.

Faith wrapped her arms around him and held

him tight, riding out the storm of passion with him and praying there would be something left of her heart when it was all over.

"Mama, I want toast," Lindy announced, kneeling on her chair at the kitchen table, her place setting overrun with tiny plastic dinosaurs.

"Yes, sweetie, I know," Faith said. She was trying simultaneously to handle the coffee maker and the toaster while keeping one eye on the eggs that were cooking on the stove.

"I'll do the coffee," Alaina volunteered as she and Jayne entered the room. She took the pot from Faith's slightly trembling hand, giving her friend a sharp, speculative glance. "You look tired. Did you get any sleep last night?"

Faith felt her cheeks flush instantly. She'd hardly slept a wink, but the reason had nothing to do with insomnia. "Um—I'm all right," she mumbled.

Blast it, couldn't she be a little more sophisticated? Did she have to blush as if Alaina had come right out and asked if she'd just spent the last six hours between the sheets with Shane Callan? And for heaven's sake, she was a grown woman. It wasn't as if Shane was the first man she'd ever gone to bed with.

He was the second.

He was the only man she'd ever made love with in the truest sense of the term—whether he admitted his heart was involved or not. She had to believe it was. Nothing that beautiful had ever come from simple physical need.

"Mama, can I have my toast now?"

"Yes, Lindy, I'm coming." She put her daughter's breakfast on a plate and dropped it off at the table on her way to check the eggs.

Lindy made a face and lifted one square of bread by the corner. "I don't want this kind."

"It's the only kind we have."

"I want the kind with raisins."

"We're all out of the raisin kind."

"Can we go to the beach today?"

"No, honey, not today," Faith said, sighing, putting the teakettle on to heat. "Mama's got work to do."

"Work, work, work," Lindy grumbled, folding her toast in half and mushing it with her fist. "All grown-ups ever do is work."

"Oh, I don't know about that, sugar plum,"

Jayne said, pausing in her task of pouring orange juice to lean across the table and tweak Lindy's nose. "Grown-ups have fun sometimes too, don't we, Faith?"

Faith couldn't have looked more guilty had she been wearing a sign around her neck that spelled out "strumpet" in big glossy red letters. "Who, me?"

Alaina's mouth lifted in a wry smile as she leaned back against the counter and crossed her arms. "I believe the question was rhetorical, not accusatory. At any rate, most kinds of fun aren't against the law, are they, Mr. Callan?"

If Faith's cheeks had been red before, they were fuchsia now as she looked up and her gaze collided with Shane's. He strolled into the kitchen looking impossibly handsome in black jeans and a gray polo shirt, his black hair glistening, wet from his shower. It seemed to Faith the look in his eyes was blatantly male and possessive as he came toward her. He didn't even glance at Alaina when he answered her.

"Like you said, counselor, a rhetorical question."

He stopped within inches of Faith—too close for his own sanity—and lifted a hand to brush his knuckles against her cheek. He had told himself in the shower that he was going to take a step back from her, cool things off a little so she could get some perspective. But his stern, cold dictates had vaporized the instant he'd walked into the kitchen. It seemed his knack for detachment couldn't hold a candle to Faith's appeal. Looking at her now, all he wanted to do was wrap her up in his arms and carry her back to bed. If he hadn't been dimly aware of their captive audience, he would have done just that.

Dammit, she brought every primitive feeling he had rushing to the surface. Every time he got within three feet of her he felt more like a caveman than a man with an Ivy League education. When Faith looked up at him the way she was doing now, her big brown eyes all soft and shining, he felt as if he were going to go up in smoke—not unlike the pan of scrambled eggs on the stove.

"Faith?"

"Hmmm?" she asked as the air seeped out of her lungs. During the long night her body had become very well acquainted with Shane's, to the point that the slightest signal from him could set off every sensual alarm she had. At the moment her whole body was humming. It was a wonder she even heard him.

"Your eggs are burning," he said with a devastatingly soft, sexy smile.

"They're not the only thing," Jayne mumbled from her ringside seat. Alaina shushed her as she slid down on a chair.

Faith's eyes rounded in shock as she turned back to her smoking pan. She yanked it off the burner and tossed the contents with a spatula to see if the food was salvageable.

"I don't want any eggs, Mama," Lindy announced as she toddled across the floor to take Shane by the hand. She sent him her sunny smile. "Come and have some toast, Shane. I'm sorry it's not the kind with raisins."

Faith managed to sit through a half hour of breakfast conversation without finishing a single piece of raisinless toast. While her friends discussed the errands they had to run and Lindy lobbied Shane for another day at the beach, Faith sipped her tea and fidgeted.

She wasn't quite certain how she was supposed to act. She'd never had a lover before. Including her husband, she added ruefully. One night with Shane made twelve years with William Gerrard pale in comparison.

"Earth to Faith. Earth to Faith," Jayne called across the table, waving a hand back and forth in front of her.

Faith jerked to attention, blushing furiously. "What? I'm sorry."

"And I thought I was the flake of the Fearsome Foursome!" Jayne drawled, shaking her head. She stared into Faith's eyes and spoke very distinctly, as if English were Faith's second language. "Honey, what are your plans for the day?"

"Oh, um, I've got book work to do, then I thought I'd put the finishing touches on the captain's suite and some of the other guest rooms."

"We could go to the beach," Lindy suggested hopefully.

"Not today, Lindy," Faith said firmly, pinning her daughter with a stern look. "Now I don't want to hear another word about it. If you're finished with your breakfast, go brush your teeth."

Sullen, Lindy gathered up her herd of plastic dinosaurs and slid down off her chair. She made the most of her exit, giving her mother a disappointed, teary-eyed glare. "When I'm a mama, I'm gonna take my babies to the beach *every* day!"

Faith heaved a sigh, propping her chin in one hand and letting the other fall to the tabletop. "Great. Now I'm Attila the Mom."

Shane reached over and gave her hand a squeeze, a move that drew not only Faith's surprised gaze but Jayne's and Alaina's as well. They all stared at him, slack-jawed. Hell, Shane thought, he was shocked himself, but the action had been automatic. It felt like the right thing to do, and he was a man who usually trusted his instincts. Swallowing down his confusion, he said, "She'll get over it."

The smile of appreciation Faith sent him hit him like a hammer between the eyes. Lord, what was the matter with him? All this woman had to do was glance at him and he damn near forgot who he was and what he was doing. And who was he to offer sage advice? What the hell did he know about kids, anyway? Nothing. He had no business offering advice. He had no business getting involved with Faith and her daughter at all. He was there to do a job.

Abruptly he pushed his chair back from the

table and stood. "I've got rounds to make," he said, suddenly all businesslike. "I have to check with my men on the perimeter."

"You might want to look in on Mr. Matthews in the caretaker's cottage," Alaina suggested dryly. "I think he and Mr. Fitz are on the brink of divorce."

"I think their karmas clash," Jayne said.

Shane didn't so much as crack a smile. He started to turn away, but Faith's voice stopped him.

"Shane," she said softly. "Thank you."

She watched him struggle to mask confused emotions. His granite will won out, and he merely gave her a curt nod, then strode purposefully out of the room. The silence he left in his wake was almost painful.

Finally Jayne cleared her throat and said delicately, "Correct me if I'm wrong here, honey, but I think we just witnessed a very significant moment."

Faith's only answer was another delicate blush. How was she supposed to explain what was going on between Shane and herself when even she wasn't certain where they were headed?

Alaina's expression was a cross between wary and worried. "I thought you didn't want to get involved with him."

"I don't seem to have a choice," Faith said, staring at the door Shane had left through. "I'm in love with him."

The captain's suite was Faith's favorite room in the inn. Located on the second floor of the Victorian part of the house, Captain Dugan's bedroom had a large window that overlooked the ocean and allowed the afternoon sun to spill in. The furniture in the room was big and masculine—a massive mahogany bed with a flat canopy of cream-and-black brocade, marble-topped tables, an enormous chest of drawers, a regal-looking William and Mary armchair with a black velvet seat cushion.

She had painted the room a rich shade of cream and accented it with pristine white and deep red. Many of the captain's personal possessions had been used as decorative pieces, including his brass-bound sea chest, which now served as a storage place for extra blankets at the foot of the bed. Adjacent to the bedroom was a luxurious bath, and beyond that was a small, comfortable sitting room. Faith was certain this suite would quickly become a favorite with patrons of the inn.

Deep in thought, she wandered around the bedroom tucking potpourri sachets into drawers, wondering what to do about Shane. When the bedroom door swung open and he stepped inside, her heart squeezed painfully at his expression. He was definitely back to being guarded and wary. Her gentle lover had vanished, slipped behind his cold wall of isolation.

"So," he said, his gaze roaming the elegantly appointed room, "this is where the infamous captain spent his nights."

"Yes. I think he still does." She managed a small laugh at the sharp glance her statement earned her. "Things get moved around in this room without my help." She motioned to a small, perfectly horrible, oil painting of a ship that hung above the dresser. "Twice I've taken that down and put it in the attic. Twice it's been back hanging on that wall the next morning. I'm told the ship in the painting was the captain's favorite."

Shane scowled at both the painting and the implication, and began prowling around the room, taking in every detail of the walls and floorboards.

Faith watched him with weary amusement. Ever the skeptic, she thought with a dying smile. He was skeptical about everything—love included. In fact, it was probably at the head of his list. She had taken hope for a few moments this morning at the breakfast table when he had reached out to give her support. Shane's concern for her had overridden his deep-seated sense of caution, but his guard had quickly slipped back into place.

Now he flipped the light on in the closet and walked in, running his fingertips along the newly painted walls, pressing gently. Faith rolled her eyes as she crossed her arms over her chest and leaned a shoulder against the doorjamb. "Shane, you've been over every inch of this house. There are no secret passages."

"I'm just doing my job."

"So you keep reminding me," she muttered, unable to keep the bitter edge from her voice.

He turned and looked at her, his gray eyes stormy. "It's best if we both remember why I'm here."

"You're right, of course," Faith said, her voice suddenly tight with unshed tears. She pushed herself away from the closet door and went to stand by the table where her sachet supplies were neatly laid out. She stared down at the squares of lace, bits of satin ribbon, and dish of fragrant rose petals and lavender, unable to work up the strength to touch any of it.

She didn't have any right to hurt, she thought. Shane had warned her he couldn't get involved. But to be perfectly honest, she had to admit the romantic in her had never quite accepted that. All along she had secretly believed giving him her love would unlock his heart and free him to love her in return.

Would she never learn?

Shane swore under his breath and left his search to follow her. He stood behind her, staring at the rigid set of her slender shoulders, willing himself not to touch her. "Faith, I don't want to hurt you."

"I know," she whispered, reaching down deep inside for a scrap of strength and wondering when that well was going to run dry. "I'm a big girl. I knew the rules going in. You don't have to worry about me. I told you I didn't expect promises. Please don't let what I said this morning ruin what time we have together."

"You didn't ruin anything," he said thickly, not surprised that his resolve was crumbling. He could no more keep from touching her than he could keep from breathing. His hands came up to cup her shoulders, his fingers gently rubbing at the tension in her muscles. "It's just . . . more complicated now."

"I'm sorry," she murmured automatically. Immediately she wanted to take the words back. What did she have to be sorry for?

"No," she said angrily, turning to face him with dark eyes blazing. "I'm tired of having to apologize. I love you, and I won't feel sorry for it. If that makes your job or your life complicated, that's just too darn bad."

Shane swore—more at the conflict within himself than at Faith. His professionalism was being torn to shreds because of his attraction to this woman. The frightening thing was that a part of him didn't give a damn. Arguments chased each other around in his head. All the while he stared down at Faith's heart-shaped face, the defiant expression she wore. Slowly logic receded until all he could focus on was the lush bow of her mouth and the heat of desire glowing inside him.

Faith trembled as Shane's hands tightened on her shoulders, his fingers biting into her flesh, burning her through the fabric of her cotton sweater. The look he wore was primitive, almost savage. His eyes held a silver light that seemed capable of boring straight through her. A muscle in his strong jaw flexed as he lowered his head toward hers.

"You make me crazy," he said, his voice little more than a growl.

Then his mouth was on hers, taking, plundering, and Faith could hear nothing but the blood pounding in her ears. The heat that flared between them burned away everything but desire. She surrendered to it immediately, melting against Shane's big hard body, her hands going up to clutch at his broad shoulders. She welcomed the thrust of his tongue, drinking in the taste of him.

For Shane arousal was instantaneous. The truth was it had never left him. Even after a night of making love with her, he wanted more. Desire had not been burned out; he had simply banked it, and now it flared up full force, searing him with an inner heat that demanded release.

He swept a hand down the curve of Faith's supple back to cup her bottom, his fingers kneading her soft flesh and gathering up the fabric of her gauzy cotton skirt. Lifting her, he pulled her hips to his, pressing her against the hard ridge of his masculinity. A deep groan rumbled up from his chest as Faith ran her leg up the outside of his thigh and squirmed to get even closer to him.

The shrill ring of the telephone brought them both back from the edge of sensual oblivion. It was on the tip of Shane's tongue to tell Faith to let the damn thing ring, but he caught himself at the last instant and stood her away from him.

This could be the call that would break the case. The case was why he was there.

Faith went to the table beside the bed, trembling so, she thought it was a wonder she couldn't hear her knees knocking together. It was simply amazing the way that man could sap the strength from her. Amazing and exciting. And frightening. Taking a deep breath, she tried to clear her head before she picked up the receiver.

"Keepsake Inn. Faith Kincaid speaking."

"Hello, Faith."

Fear shot through her like a bolt of lightning at the sound of the too-familiar whisper. She jerked around to face Shane, pale and wide-eyed, her heart pounding. His face grim, he came forward and took her free hand, his strong grasp offering her support and comfort.

"Have you seen the error of your ways?"

Trying to draw strength from Shane's steady gaze, Faith swallowed down the knot in her throat and said, "I'm going to testify."

"That's a bad decision, sweet. You know I'm watching you, don't you? You and your darling daughter. You wouldn't want anything bad to happen to little Lindy, now would you?"

Faith's stomach rolled over at the thought of this faceless monster even knowing about Lindy. It was hard enough that this ugliness should intrude on her own life, but for it to touch Lindy in any way . . . she couldn't bear the idea.

"I could take her and kill her. I could take her anytime I want."

Abruptly it was all too much. The tension that had been building over the course of this terrorism crested with the power of a tidal wave, sweeping Faith's control away. "Stop it!" she screamed into the phone. "Just stop it! Leave us alone!"

She slammed down the receiver, her face wet with tears as she turned and was met by Shane's solid form. She sagged against him like a rag doll as he pulled her into his embrace, his arms banding around her like steel.

"What did he say?"

"Lindy," she said between choking sobs. A fresh wave of fear surged through her. She tried to push herself away from Shane, but he held firm. "Please," she begged, struggling in his grasp. "I have to see Lindy."

Shane released her. Matthews would have the conversation on tape. It seemed much more important at the moment to let Faith go to her daughter. He followed her down the grand staircase, anger rolling in his gut. When he got his hands on the bastard who was doing this to her...

"Lindy!" Faith called, running down the hall to her daughter's bedroom. Terror slammed into her anew when she found the room empty and silent, the only movement the curtains stirring in the breeze. "Lindy?"

Her questioning call was met with ominous silence.

"Lindy!" she yelled, panic clawing at her as she recalled the words *I could take her and kill her.* The fear that exploded inside her was absolute and all consuming and more terrible than anything she had ever experienced or even imagined. Her child was missing.

She nearly screamed when Shane's hands closed on her shoulders and he gave her a shake. "Faith, calm down," he ordered.

"I can't find Lindy," she choked out, her eyes wild. "Shane, I can't find my daughter. He said he'd kill her. He said he'd kill my baby!"

Shane called on the cool professionalism he was known for. "We'll find her, honey. She's probably playing in some other part of the house or out in the yard. He can't get to her here."

"He said he'd kill her," Faith repeated, anguish tearing her apart inside. How could anyone be so vicious as to hurt an innocent child? "She's just a baby."

"We'll find her," Shane promised. "He can't get to her, Faith."

They searched the house. Faith, Shane, Agent Matthews, and Mr. Fitz went over every inch of the sprawling mix of structures that made up the inn. They found no trace of Lindy.

Shane's anxiety grew as they moved outside and went through the outbuildings on the property. Sweet, trusting Lindy. If that monster or some accomplice of his had somehow slipped through their security and gotten close to her, she would never have thought to be frightened.

The search party met on the lawn on the north side of the house. Fitz tugged anxiously at his gray beard. Matthews looked grim. Faith was on the verge of hysteria. Shane took her in his arms, needing to comfort her and not giving a damn about what his fellow agent would think.

"We'll find her," he said, half shouting to be heard above the wind and the sound of the sea crashing against the beach below them.

The beach.

His heart pounding, Shane bolted for the edge of the cliff and the wooden steps that snaked down it. He hit the beach running, sand kicking up behind him. Frantically his eyes scanned the area. For the first time in a long, long time he started praying, praying that Lindy hadn't fallen over the cliff or wandered too close to the surf and been swept out by the treacherous waves this coast was known for.

Then he spotted her. He stopped in his tracks, air sawing in and out of his lungs like hot razors. Lindy sat in the sand, half-hidden behind a boulder, playing happily with her herd of plastic dinosaurs. Her ever-present doll was propped up against the rock, watching the proceedings with one eye stuck shut. She danced her dinosaurs around a lopsided sand castle, all the while singing at the top of her lungs "Don't Worry, Be Happy."

Relief rolled over Shane with all the power of the waves that were crashing against the shore fifty feet away, leaving him so weak he nearly went down on his knees. Lindy looked up at him suddenly, and a smile lit up her pixie face like a sunbeam.

"Hi, Shane! Did you come to play with me?"

He couldn't answer her for the knot in his throat.

Faith ran across the sand, her legs feeling like lead, her lungs on fire. She pushed past Shane and dropped down in the midst of the dinosaurs, scooping her daughter into her arms. Sobbing, she hugged Lindy until the little girl squirmed.

"Oh, baby, you're safe!" With a shaking hand she brushed at her child's silky red-gold curls. "I was so scared!"

Lindy's lip quivered as she looked at her mother. "Don't cry, Mama. I don't like it when you cry."

Faith tried to smile and laugh, but in the end all she could do was hold her baby close and let go of all the tears fear had built inside her.

"I could have lost her."

Faith sat on the edge of Lindy's bed, watching her daughter sleep, running her fingertips over her child's hair. Hours had passed since the crisis of the afternoon, and still the fear lay just under the facade of her calm, threatening to erupt at any second.

She felt as if something had shattered both inside her and around her. The last of her sense of safety had been fragmented. Through all of this hideous business the one thing Faith had clung to was the knowledge that she would always have Lindy. Now that too had been snatched away from her.

She'd been forced to realize that Lindy could be taken away. In the blink of an eye her child could be gone. It hadn't happened today. Today Lindy had simply taken herself to the beach. But that didn't mean it wouldn't happen in the future. Faith could still hear that evil silky voice promising to kill the most important person in her life—her child. A shudder snaked through her body and tears welled up in her eyes yet again.

"I love her so much," she murmured brokenly. "I'd die if something happened to her."

"She's all right, Faith," Shane said softly. With a gentle grip he took her arm and drew her up from the bed and gathered her close against him, not bothering to wonder where all this tenderness was coming from. "We'll make sure nothing happens to her. She'll have a full-time babysitter from now on. And tomorrow you're having a fence installed with a locked gate at the top of those steps."

Faith looked up at him, her expression so bleak it nearly broke his heart. As the tears slipped past her dark lashes and spilled down her cheeks, she said, "I've never been so scared."

"I know."

He knew because the same fear had raked its talons through him, the force of it leaving him shaken. Not so long ago Shane had thought himself incapable of caring that deeply. He had believed the job had robbed him of that basic human quality, but he'd been wrong.

He ran a hand into Faith's tangled curls and eased her head to his chest where she wept silently, her tears soaking into his shirt. She felt so small in his arms, so fragile, so in need of his protection.

"Come on, honey," he murmured, leading her toward the door that connected her room to Lindy's. "You need to get some rest."

Reluctantly Faith went with him. She was so exhausted she couldn't think straight. Shane was probably right, she needed rest. But the thought of being alone with her fear made her throat tighten convulsively.

"Don't leave me," she whispered.

Quietly closing and locking the door that connected the two rooms, Shane turned to face her. With no thought about professionalism or detachment or objectivity, he took her in his arms and hugged her. Rubbing his cheek against the top of her head, he whispered, "I won't leave you."

He bent his head and softly kissed the remnants of her tears from her pale cheeks. Faith murmured his name, her trembling hands running up and down the bulging muscles of his arms. He was so strong, so solid, and he possessed the power to make her forget everything. In his arms she could lose herself, she could escape.

She tilted her face up, her trembling mouth capturing his in a kiss that was as soft and fragile as a rose petal. When she spoke, the plea was in her eyes as well as her voice. "Make love to me, Shane. Please. I need you."

Shane's heart ached as he looked down at her. He didn't question her need or her motives. In truth he needed this union as badly as Faith did. She needed to lose herself in the sweetness of their lovemaking. He needed to comfort her and reassure himself that she was safe, that she was his to care for and protect.

They came together not in a blaze of passion, but with exquisite tenderness and a deep hunger that each sought to prolong. Faith savored every kiss, every caress, blocking her mind to everything but her need to be loved by this man. She focused on the incredible sensations he aroused in her body as he lavished attention on her breasts with his mouth and probed the honeyed warmth between her thighs with his gentle musician's fingers. Desire built slowly over the foundation of desperation, until she felt encompassed by it.

"Shane." She groaned his name as her finger-nails raked the hard muscles of his back. "Now. Please take me now."

At her command he slid into her in one power-ful thrust, filling the tight hot sheath of her wom-anhood, reaching deep to stroke the very center of her need. Faith let go the last tattered threads of her control. Wrapping her legs around his lean hips, she surged upward beneath him, meeting his powerful thrusts and begging for more, begging for the ecstasy that would blind her to all else.

Shane felt the end rushing toward them. He wrapped one strong arm around Faith, lifting her so that her nipples burrowed through his chest hair to rub against his burning flesh. He brushed her damp hair back from her face and kissed her deeply, al-most wildly, thrusting his tongue into her mouth in the same rhythm as he thrust himself between her legs, branding her as his in the most basic way he could.

Faith's hands stroked down his back to his hips, her fingers digging into the tight muscles of his but-tocks. With one last stroke he took her over the edge, and the inner pulsing that signaled her fulfill-ment triggered his. A hoarse cry tearing from his throat, Shane arched against her and spilled himself in her.

"I love you," Faith whispered as Shane's body relaxed on top of her, his weight bearing down on her with a delicious warmth. Her lips brushed across the roughness of his evening beard as she murmured the words again, then fell into a deep, exhausted sleep.

Shane raised up on one elbow above her and studied her face in the soft light from the bedside lamp. *I love you.* He didn't say the words aloud, but they reverberated throughout his whole being. Despite all his warnings he had fallen in love with Faith Kincaid.

He'd never felt so vulnerable in his life. And, at the same time, the truth warmed him. After years of living in cold gray shadows, Faith's love was reaching out to him like a beacon. This sweet, good woman was offering him a chance to start over, and every weary corner of his warrior's heart wanted to accept.

It felt as if he were standing on a threshold with the darkness of his past behind him and the possibility of a future with Faith before him. Faith was standing in that doorway as well. Their pasts were intertwined now, and until they could shut that door, until this case was over, their future would have to wait.

Still, Shane thought as Faith cuddled close against him, he had a future, and for the first time in a long time it didn't look bleak or empty.

NINE

"WE TRACED THE call to a phone booth in Mendocino," Shane reported, drumming his fingertips on the computer printout that lay on the table before him.

"And?" John Banks prompted, his typically sardonic tone not made any more pleasant by the fact that he'd dragged himself out of bed and onto a plane at the crack of dawn. His thick head of steel gray hair was so unruly, he looked as though he had come through a wind tunnel. He needed a shave. His disposition was as rumpled as the dark suit that covered his sturdy frame.

"No distinguishable prints. Fiber evidence isn't worth a damn at this point—a hundred people go in and out of that phone booth every day."

"Wonderful." Banks pulled off his glasses to rub at the bridge of his big nose. Replacing them, he stabbed Shane with a pointed look.

"He's playing games with us," Shane said. "Each of the letters he's sent has a different postmark. Each of the calls we've managed to trace has been from a different town—all within a fifty-mile radius. We've got them on tape, but his voice is either too muffled or mechanically altered to make them of any use."

"Suggestions?"

"I want Faith and Lindy moved to a safe house," Shane said in a tone of voice that did not invite an opposing opinion. He took a strong pull on his cigarette and leveled his gaze at Faith, daring her to defy his plan.

They had been over this already. At three o'clock in the morning. Shane had awakened to find Faith pacing back and forth beside her bed, anxious and angry over the situation her ex-husband had embroiled her in and the feelings of helplessness that had all but overwhelmed her.

Now they sat at one of the larger tables in the inn's dining room with afternoon light streaming in through the tall windows. The setting was different, but it was quite clear by the angle of Faith's chin that the argument was going to be the same. Under all her sweetness, behind those gorgeous brown eyes the lady had a true Irish temper.

The door to the kitchen swung open, and Alaina and Jayne walked in, Alaina looking very official with her dark hair pulled back and black-rimmed glasses framing her arctic blue eyes. Jayne's expression was one of wide-eyed intensity, as if she had just been thrust into a scene in a movie. Shane bristled at the intrusion, but Faith cut him off before he could voice his objection.

"I asked Alaina and Jayne to sit in on this meeting," she said. Shane shot a burning look her way. Her slim shoulders stiffened, and she stuck her chin out a little farther. "Alaina is my attorney, and Jayne is . . . well . . . Jayne is my friend."

"And spiritual confidant," Jayne added, sliding down on a chair.

Shane rolled his eyes. Banks frowned, but it was hard to discern whether he was frowning at the addition to the powwow or at Jayne's outfit—a wildly flowered dirndl skirt that hung to her dainty ankles and an oversize Notre Dame T-shirt, the end of which was tied in a knot at her waist.

"As I was saying," Shane began in a tight voice, when the door swung open again and Mr. Fitz marched in.

"Here I am, as ye asked, lassie," he said, nodding purposefully to Faith as he tugged on the bottom of his smelly brown coat.

The glower Shane turned on her was almost enough to make Faith swallow her bravado. "Are you the least familiar with the concept of the need-to-know basis?" he questioned in a dark, silky voice.

"Um . . . Mr. Fitz lives here," she said, not wanting to admit she had wanted all these people present for moral support more than anything. "He needs to know."

Shane's hands clenched the edge of the table like vise clamps as he struggled with his temper. "Why don't we just call the Anastasia *Gazette* and tell them everything that's going on here?"

Faith sniffed. "You don't have to get snippy."

"I'm drawing the line here, Faith," Shane said

through his teeth. He turned to the bearded, bedraggled caretaker. "You can go, Mr. Fitz. You *don't* need to know."

The old man's beetle brows waggled furiously as he gave Shane a hard stare, then turned and left, grumbling under his breath.

"Can we get on with this, please?" Banks asked pointedly.

"Yes." Shane turned toward Faith once again and gave her a direct order. "Pack what you need. We're moving you out of here."

"No." She watched Shane blow smoke out of his nose and wondered how much of it could be attributed to his mood rather than his cigarette. He didn't like her plan, but her mind was made up. She was all through playing this hellish waiting game. The scare she'd had over Lindy's disappearance the day before had pushed her to take the offensive. Her chin came up a notch, and she turned toward Banks, meeting his bloodshot green eyes with a fierce look.

"I want the man caught. I want him punished."

Banks opened his mouth to comment, but Shane ignored his boss. All his attention was focused on the woman he had just discovered that he loved. "I want you safe, Faith."

"That's what I want too," Faith insisted, her eyes begging him to understand. "I can't go on like this, living in a state of terror, waiting and waiting. I can't go on letting William Gerrard victimize me."

Shane's stubborn expression didn't alter a fraction. "Then we'll put you in a safe house until the trial is over."

"And then what? What do I do if you never catch this madman? Am I supposed to go on forever waiting for William's accomplice to take revenge?"

She wasn't going to like his next suggestion, Shane knew, but it was the only foolproof solution. It was the solution the frightened man inside him wanted put into motion immediately—anything to keep Faith safe. The idea of anyone hurting her or Lindy scared the hell out of him. "Then we put you in the witness protection program."

"Absolutely not. This inn is my home, Shane, my dream. I came here with my friends to start a new life. I will not let William steal that from me. When I left him, I vowed I would never let him manipulate me again. That's exactly what I'd be doing if

I went into hiding. I want this ended now." She turned back toward Banks. "I want to set a trap."

Again when Banks opened his mouth to offer an opinion, Shane jumped in ahead of him. His low, rough voice had the razor edge of steel in it, which matched the glint in his gray eyes perfectly. He brought Faith's attention back to himself by snatching hold of her wrist, as if he thought he could change her mind with the strength of his grip. "No way in hell am I letting you set yourself up as bait."

Faith glared up at him, her dark eyes blazing. "Isn't that what I've been all along?"

Shane ground his teeth. He couldn't deny it. From the beginning the plan had been to construct a loose net around Faith in order to capture the missing piece from the DataScam puzzle. The difference—the very big difference—was that Shane hadn't been in love with Mrs. William Gerrard, the woman he had been sent here to watch over. He was very much in love with Faith Kincaid, the woman who had quietly stolen her way into his heart over the past few weeks.

It went against everything in him to allow her to put herself in danger. In fact, the idea terrified him. It was the kind of fear that reached deep inside, past all his barriers to the lonely man who had distanced himself from others all these years. He hated the feeling, hated the way it interfered with his logic.

"What you're talking about is entirely different." He fairly growled the words as he ground out his cigarette on the delicate china saucer before him.

Faith met his fierce gaze without flinching. A corner of her mind was aware that Shane's attitude was stemming from something other than professional judgment, but she couldn't wonder about that right now. This was not the time for romantic fantasies. It was time for her to take control of her fate. "What I'm talking about is putting an end to this so I can get on with my life."

"If we follow your damn fool plan, you may not have a life to get on with!" Trying to dominate her with his size, he leaned over her until they were practically nose to nose. Faith didn't so much as blink.

"I'm with Shane," Alaina announced. Faith's expression clearly branded her a traitor, but that didn't sway Alaina's judgment. "You're under no obligation to help catch this person, Faith. The burden of his arrest is on the government, as is your right to protection. As your legal counsel and your friend, I advise against your scheme."

"Well, I'm with Faith," Jayne said, always ready to stick up for the underdog. "A person can live in suspense for only so long—about the length of a Hitchcock movie. This has already gone on too long. And if Faith strongly feels it's her destiny to help capture this man . . . well, then maybe it's just her karma," she said with a decisive nod. She gave Faith her most supportive look. "As long as there's a hundred cops around and no chance of you getting hurt, I think it's a good idea."

Alaina slanted her a look. "This from someone who thought mood rings were a good idea."

"They were," Jayne grumbled, crossing her arms over her meager bosom. "Just because yours was always black—"

"May I interject a thought here?" Banks questioned dryly, raising his big square hands in supplication. "After all, I did just fly the width of the continent to be in on this discussion."

Shane shot his boss a glare of pure annoyance. "What?"

"I think Ms. Kincaid has a point."

Shane's answer to that was a rude snort. He slumped back in his chair like a sulky teenager and scowled at Faith. "I think Ms. Kincaid has a screw loose."

Faith's temper boiled over abruptly. She was operating on too much anxiety and too little sleep. Her chair scraped back against the polished wood floor as she pushed herself to her feet.

"Just what is your problem?" she demanded, bracing her small hands on the tabletop and leaning over Shane for a change. "You came here perfectly willing to use me as cheese to trap this rat. Now that I'm willing to play an active part in your plan, you suddenly want to put me under lock and key! It doesn't make any sense!"

Shane shoved his own chair back from the table and stood, regaining his considerable height advantage.

"It doesn't have to make sense," he declared, his voice a menacing purr as he moved a step closer to her, his hands jammed at the waistband of his gray trousers.

Faith leaned toward him, heedless of the muscle twitching in his rock-solid jaw. They'd been arguing this same point for hours, never getting past it. She'd had it with his wall of arrogant reserve.

"Why?" she prodded, bent on breaking that cool control of his and getting a straight answer out of him. She inched ahead until the toes of her small canvas sneakers butted up against Shane's black loafers. "Because you're in charge? Because you're on some typically male power trip that dictates you have to have control over a mere woman? Because—"

"Because I'm in love with you, dammit!" he bellowed.

The room went suddenly, utterly still. Faith was certain she could hear the dust motes settling on the furniture. She stared at Shane with her mouth hanging open as his words sank in. He was in love with her. He was in love with her, but he didn't appear to be very happy about it. Well, she thought, her head swimming, that definitely gave them something in common.

John Banks cleared his throat discreetly, breaking the tense silence. Faith hauled a deep breath into her lungs as she stepped away from the confrontation, her cheeks turning pink. Shane's broad shoulders sagged as he forced the tension from his muscles. He stared down at the floor, not quite able to believe he had just blurted out his deepest feelings—in front of witnesses, no less.

"Agent Callan," Banks said neutrally as he rose from his chair, brushing ineffectually at his wrinkled suit, "may I speak with you in private?"

Without a word or a glance for anyone, Shane turned on his heel and led the way out through the French doors onto the stone terrace. He stalked to the farthest corner and faced the sea as he lit another cigarette, noting with grim amusement that his hands were shaking.

Dammit, he was losing it completely, losing his edge, losing his perspective...losing his heart... losing his mind.

"I should have taken the R and R," he said, wryly referring to the advice his boss had given him after the Silvanus bust.

Banks leaned back against the stone wall that surrounded the terrace, his tired eyes calmly studying his best agent. "What? And miss all this fun?"

Shane shot him a venomous look that had the older man chuckling wearily and mumbling under his breath, "The bigger they are..."

Sidestepping the comment, Shane went back to what the professional in him considered the heart of the matter—the case. "I won't let her play bait in this game."

"She's serious about ending this thing, Shane. She wouldn't have called me in otherwise."

"I don't care how serious she is. She's not calling the shots here; she's a civilian."

"Yes, she's a civilian. Meaning she doesn't have to take orders from us. If she wants to walk down the main street of Anastasia and invite this creep to take a shot at her, you couldn't do a damn thing to stop her."

Shane's eyes narrowed and glittered dangerously as he said, "You want to make a bet?"

"What are you going to do?" Banks asked with a sarcastic laugh. "Hit her over the head with your dinosaur bone and carry her off to your cave? This is the modern era, pal. Ladies have minds of their own, believe me. Besides, she does have a say in this; it's her life we're tinkering with."

Looking every inch like a cornered panther, Shane wheeled on the man who knew him better than anyone. "I mean it, John. I won't have her put in any more danger than she's already in."

Banks didn't flinch at the outburst, didn't blink.

"What's the problem here, Shane? What Faith is proposing is our original scenario taken just one step further. We're dealing with a single player, a single variable who may or may not be dangerous. So far he's been long on threats and short on action."

Shane gave a harsh laugh. "That's supposed to make it okay? He hasn't actually killed her yet, so we should give him one good shot at it—just in case he's really serious?"

Ignoring the sarcasm, Banks pressed on. "We can make certain he won't have a chance of getting to her."

Shane's jaw clenched as he turned to stare out at the ocean again. His voice was low and strained. "There's always a chance."

For a long moment the only sound was that of the ocean pounding the shore a hundred feet below. The wind whipped at Banks's wildly mussed hair as he turned and leaned his forearms on top of the stone wall. "This isn't Quantico, Shane," he said softly, his voice almost gentle. "She's not Ellie."

Shane's heart clenched at the comparison. He had loved Ellie Adamson. He had lost her because his emotions had clouded his judgment. Now he prayed his old friend and colleague was right, because he knew with bleak certainty that if he lost Faith, he would lose everything. She was his hope, his salvation, his one slim chance at a future that wasn't empty. What he felt for her was so intense, it was like a fire in his soul where for so long there had been nothing but cold and darkness.

"We'll do it her way." Banks made the announcement, then took a deep breath and changed the subject. "Rumor has it Strauss bought a boat in Mazatlan. Looks like he's taking his act south after all."

"Yeah," Shane commented absently, not really listening. His gaze had fallen on Faith as she came through the French doors and onto the terrace.

He loved her. He'd forgotten how painful love could be. It was a relentless ache inside him— knowing he loved her and being terrified of losing her.

How had such an innocent woman become entangled in such a dangerous situation? Faith didn't belong in the world of espionage. Of course, Shane acknowledged the irony, he never would have met her otherwise. Bitterly he wondered if they wouldn't have both been better off. Certainly she would have been.

"If you'll excuse me, Ms. Kincaid," Banks said, straightening away from the wall. He smoothed his hands over the lapels of his hopelessly rumpled suit and gave Faith a wry smile. "I believe I'll go freshen up before we discuss this further."

"Of course," Faith murmured, her eyes on Shane as his boss made his exit.

"You're getting your wish," he said flatly, tossing down his cigarette and grinding it against the flagstone with his shoe.

Faith wondered if he realized the thing she had wished for most was his love. He was giving her that, albeit begrudgingly—but it was a start at least. The next step was to close the door on her past so they could be free to look for a future together. It was clear by Shane's stony expression that her idea for achieving that end was the wish he was talking about.

She folded her arms over her chest as the wind cut through the yellow Shaker sweater she wore. "It's the best way."

His expression incredulous, Shane barked a laugh. "You're an expert?"

Faith met his angry gaze, though tears rose in her eyes. She was all through backing away from trouble, even when it came in a six-foot-four-inch package. "I'm an expert at feeling helpless and afraid and manipulated. I have to put an end to that, Shane. Please understand."

He stared at her for a long moment, unable to reconcile the conflicts within himself. She was asking for his support, but he was simply too afraid to give it to her. She wanted to risk her life and have his blessing to do it. Anger burned in his chest. How dare she make him love her, then ask him to let her get killed. Dammit, why couldn't she have left his heart alone? That was where he belonged—alone, in the shadows.

Emotions roiling inside him like an angry sea, he said, "Do what you want."

Faith squeezed her eyes shut against the pain and held her breath as she listened to him walk away.

It wasn't a bad evening by coastal standards, Faith thought as she wandered away from the house, strolling through the lush grass twenty yards in from the edge of the cliff. Clouds had rolled in, promising rain later on, but the fog bank that was such a constant this time of year was nothing more than wisps tonight. Bits of it floated past her like thin strips of cotton candy. She tucked her hands into the pockets of her cardigan, hunched her shoulders against the chill, and walked on.

Dinner had come and gone, a vague memory of frozen pizza eaten during the discussion of the case. Setting a trap to catch the man terrorizing her had been Faith's idea, but she remembered little of the conversation. Shane had occupied her attention almost to the exclusion of all else.

Her heart ached—not so much because of him as *for* him. He'd declared his love for her, but there was little doubt in her mind he would sooner have cut out his tongue. Immediately he had withdrawn from her—physically and emotionally—pulling back behind those gray granite walls of his. The tension that had thickened the air between them since that moment had driven her out of the house.

Oh, it wasn't Shane alone, she admitted as her steps led her down a gentle slope toward the caretaker's cottage. It was everything—Shane, the case, thoughts of her life with William, memories of the Fearsome Foursome and their days at Notre Dame. All of it had crowded in on her until she'd begun to feel claustrophobic. As soon as she had tucked Lindy in and watched her daughter drift off to sleep, she had slipped out a side door in search of fresh air and solitude.

She let her mind drift now to thoughts of her friends—Alaina and Jayne and Bryan. Their lives had taken such different paths. The dreams they had shared with one another had been altered or left behind or attained, only to discover there was no gold at the end of the rainbow. More than a decade had passed since they had each rushed off with youthful enthusiasm to find their futures. Life had led three of them to meet once again at the same crossroads, and together they had chosen the path that had brought them to Anastasia, to what had once been a fantasy dreamed up by college kids on spring break.

What did the future hold for her now, Faith wondered as she stopped to look out at the sea that was as gray as liquid pewter. Absently she rubbed her keepsake between her thumb and forefinger, and her thoughts turned back to Shane.

He wasn't an easy man to love, but love him she did with all her heart. Could they have a future together? He'd told her from the start he couldn't make promises. A man like Shane was married to his profession, and it was a profession that demanded he be a loner. It was a profession that had locked a tender, sensitive man behind walls of cynicism.

She had to hope that after all this madness was past, she would be able to convince Shane the time had come for him to let go of the shadows shrouding his soul, because she was convinced right down to her toes that he was the man she had been waiting for forever. They could have a life together there at Keepsake, a nice, quiet life. And a family. Tingles fizzed through her like champagne bubbles at the thought of carrying Shane's baby, of holding it and nursing it at her breast while Shane looked on, proud and content.

Turning away from the ocean, she let her gaze wander over the lovely, rolling land that belonged to her, to the eccentric complex of houses that made up her inn. Due west of her, beyond her long driveway and to the other side of the road, the wild meadowland gave way abruptly to rugged hills beautifully cloaked in deep green forest that looked nearly black now in the fading light. And just a few yards to the north of where she stood sat the caretaker's cottage—a small whitewashed stone building with a slate roof and a bright red door. It marked the northern border of her property with a distinctively Irish flare.

Yes, this would be a perfect place to raise a family. It would be a perfect place for Shane to settle and shed the shell he'd encased his tender feelings in to protect them from a world of grim reality. Faith closed her eyes and pictured the scenes clearly in her mind, praying with all her might that she wasn't just wasting her time romanticizing, letting her heart chase rainbows.

She checked her watch and heaved a sigh. It was time to head back to the house. Banks wanted to go over the particulars of their plan once again. But as long as she was so close, she decided she would stop in to check on Agent Matthews first. The poor guy had scarcely been allowed to set foot out of the cottage because he was the expert when it came to the phone tap and that was where his equipment had been set up. She bit her lip and winced at the thought of having to share living space with the noisome, irascible Mr. Fitz. Del Matthews deserved some kind of commendation for sacrifice above and beyond the call of duty.

Bringing her fist up to knock at the door, Faith frowned when it moved inward on its hinges as she applied pressure. "Mr. Matthews?" she called as she stuck her head inside.

The place seemed dead quiet. The lights had not been turned on. Shadows swallowed up all the corners of the cluttered living room, giving the place an eerie cast. The furniture was old and worn. Books were jammed haphazardly into a built-in case in one wall. An angry-looking steelhead trout stared down at her from its mount above the cold stone fireplace.

"Mr. Matthews?" Faith called again, inching her way inside. "Mr. Fitz?"

Silence was her answer. Gooseflesh rippled the skin on her arms, but she ignored it and continued on into the cottage.

She found Matthews in the small main-floor

bedroom sitting with his back to the door, monitoring his machines, earphones clamped on his head. Faith breathed a sigh of relief, only briefly wondering why he hadn't turned on a light.

"There you are," she said, crossing the room. She stopped beside his chair, but the questions that had formed in her mind never made it any farther than her throat. She tapped Del Matthews on the shoulder, and his body suddenly slumped sideways and sprawled onto the floor at her feet.

Faith clamped a hand to her chest as if to keep her racing heart from leaping out. For just an instant she froze as her mind absorbed the visual information. Del Matthews was dead. Realizing that, she took two steps backward, ready to whirl and run. She had to get to Shane.

"How thoughtful of you to come down to the cottage, Faith," a dark, silky voice murmured in her ear. "You've saved me a great deal of trouble."

At the sound of that voice every muscle in her body tensed with a speed and intensity that was painful. She didn't have to turn around to know it was the barrel of a gun she felt pressing into her spine. The metallic taste of fear washed through her mouth. The need to see her tormentor surged through her but was overridden by the feel of the pistol in her back. The sensation of a weight crushing her chest reminded her to start breathing again, though the tension in her muscles prevented much more than a shallow gasp.

"Who are you? Why are you doing this?" she asked, managing nothing more than a raw whisper.

"Why, I'm an old friend of Agent Callan's," he said, sarcasm edging his curiously pleasant, well-modulated tone. "My name is Adam Strauss."

TEN

SHANE SAT AT the piano, playing softly. As he had time and again in his past, he let the music sort his feelings through for him.

He loved Faith Kincaid. Damned if he hadn't wanted to throttle her for it earlier in the day, but he was getting used to the idea now. What he wasn't comfortable with was the plan to use her openly as bait to catch a possible killer.

It might have been a different story if they'd had a better handle on their perpetrator, but they didn't have a clue as to who the man might be, what his connection to Gerrard was, what his background was. The guy might have been a mild-mannered former mail clerk from DataTech, or he might have been a hired gun. Whoever he was, he hadn't taken one false step. Shane couldn't shake the feeling that the man was a pro.

The thought of setting Faith up for the creep made his blood run cold.

But they would deal with it. The decision had been made, and he would follow orders. But he vowed he would bring Faith through this without so much as a scratch. No harm was going to come to the woman he loved—not if he had anything to say about it. And when it was over, he was going to tell her he loved her—not shout it at her, not say it as if it were a curse, but whisper it to her, kiss the words across her skin, give voice to the feelings that had invaded his previously empty soul.

He was going to make love to her until there was no doubt in her mind about his feelings for her. The future still held uncertainties, but there was one thing he was feeling more and more sure of—he wanted that future to include Faith . . .

"Hi, Shane."

. . . and Lindy.

Shane's fingers stilled on the keys, and he turned,

his heart warming instantly at the sight of little Lindy standing beside the piano bench in her Care Bears pajamas. She had a choke hold on her doll with her right arm and was rubbing at her sleepy eyes with her other hand.

"What are you doing out of bed, honey?" he asked softly, not even trying to stop himself from reaching out to brush at the little girl's tousled blond curls.

Without waiting for an invitation, Lindy scrambled up onto the padded bench and situated herself on Shane's lap. "I had a bad dream about dinosaurs. Where's my mama?"

"I don't know." He and Faith had gone their separate ways after dinner in a tacit agreement to cool off before they discussed the case further. "Isn't she with Alaina and Jayne?"

Lindy shook her head, an earnest expression on her face as she stared up at him with her thumb inching toward her mouth. "Huh-uh."

A sliver of fear skimmed his nerves, but Shane dismissed it. There was no danger. Faith wouldn't have left the property, and the property was under surveillance.

"I want my mama 'cause I need a hug real bad,"

Lindy said soberly. Her lower lip plumped out, and her brow furrowed with the threat of oncoming tears.

Letting go a little more of his reserve, Shane scooped her up in his arms and held her tight, deeply inhaling Lindy's warm, powder-soft scent. "How about if I give you a good hug now, and then we'll go together and find your mama?"

Lindy hooked one arm around his neck and squeezed for all she was worth. "Okie-dokie, but I still get a hug from Mama too."

"Deal."

Faith wasn't in her office or her bedroom or his bedroom or the kitchen. Shane had to fight to keep the cold wave of fear from sweeping over him as he carried Lindy through the rambling old house. The place had twenty-seven rooms and four attics. Faith could be anywhere, putzing around with decorating details or hunting through old trunks left behind by long-dead residents. She liked to do that kind of thing when she was nervous or angry.

Maybe she had gone upstairs to search for that ridiculous ghost she believed so strongly in. His brain spewed out a dozen possible simple explanations for her disappearance, while the sixth sense he had relied on so many times over the years told him with ever-increasing volume that something was very wrong.

One thing was certain. When he found her, he was going to take her in his arms and not let go of her until morning. He kicked himself mentally for having been such a bastard about the case. He could understand her need to end it, to try to get back some control over her life. He could have shown her that understanding instead of snarling at her like a wounded lion. He would—just as soon as he found her.

They had been through a dozen rooms when Shane realized Lindy had fallen asleep in his arms. He gently tucked her into her bed, brushed a kiss to her cheek, and slipped back out into the hall, quietly closing the door behind him. When he turned, he was met by a grim-faced John Banks.

Immediately Shane's pulse picked up a beat. "What is it?"

"We need to talk."

They stepped into Faith's office, and Banks closed the door.

"Matthews is dead," he said in a tight voice.

The words set off an explosion of panic in Shane's

chest. He stared at his boss, praying to God he'd heard wrong. "What?"

"He's dead. The caretaker found him. Timmons and Cerini are at the scene now. Where's Faith?"

Dragging his hands back through his hair, Shane swore viciously. "I don't know. I can't find her."

The silence that hung between the two men was as brittle as spun glass; the ringing of the telephone shattered it.

Swallowing down the knot in his throat, Shane grabbed up the receiver. "Callan."

Everything inside him turned to ice at the sound of the voice on the other end of the line. It was cultured, sardonic, and deadly. "Shane, my old friend. Long time no see."

"Strauss."

Adam Strauss chuckled, a sound that managed to embody evil rather than humor. "And here I thought perhaps you had forgotten me."

"Never." Cradling the receiver between his shoulder and ear, Shane pulled his gun from his shoulder holster and checked the clip.

"That's a comfort. I certainly haven't forgotten about you, dear friend. In fact, I'm rather anxious to see you. As is Ms. Kincaid."

Adam Strauss had Faith. In a terrible flash of insight Shane realized he had never truly known terror until this moment. Now it threatened to swallow him whole. Adam Strauss was a cold-blooded killer, a man without a soul, and he had Faith.

Questions about Faith's status roared through his head, but Shane forced himself not to ask them. Showing an interest in her would only make her situation more tenuous... if it wasn't too late already. Pushing the thought to the back of his mind he tried to concentrate on keeping the conversation going, all the while straining to catch background noises that could give him a clue as to where Strauss was.

"I heard you'd gone to Argentina."

"Tsk, tsk," Strauss said mockingly. "After everything we went through together, you didn't really think I'd leave without saying good-bye, did you?"

"No," Shane admitted. "I didn't."

"You and I have a little unfinished business to take care of, *mon ami*."

"Where are you?"

The laughter that floated over the phone lines rang with rich amusement. "Nice try, Agent Callan, but I'd rather not have an army of your compadres descending on our little soiree. What we have to settle is between you and me."

"Why the theatrics with the Kincaid woman, then?" he asked, fighting to keep emotion out of his voice. He holstered his pistol and wiped a sweating palm on the leg of his pants. "She's got nothing to do with this."

"Doesn't she? Ah, well, you know me, Shane. I always have had a flare for the dramatic. Remember our foray into the theater district that time—"

"Can the bull, Strauss," Shane cut him off. He wanted no reminders of his time inside the Silvanus operation. He'd come too close to the edge, too close to losing what it was that made him human rather than a cunning, vicious animal like Adam Strauss. Now he forced a sigh and a bored tone. "I've had a long day. Where do you want to meet?"

"Testy tonight, aren't we?" Strauss taunted lazily, then turned businesslike. "I'll give you ten minutes to drive to Anastasia, to the phone booth outside Dylan's Bar and Bait Shop. I'll call you there and give you further instructions."

Shane swore at his nemesis in disgust. "You've seen too many Dirty Harry movies."

"Don't be insulting, Irish," Strauss said on a

laugh. "Oh, and need I remind you?" he added as an afterthought. "Come alone."

Shane stared blindly at the stretch of road that was illuminated by nothing more than the head-lights of the car. The night was as black as the heart of the killer he was on his way to meet.

The road dipped and curved, turned and cut back along the cliff edge. Frequent signs advised caution and a prudent speed limit. He ignored them. The sedan hugged the pavement, though its driver was operating on nothing more than reflexes and sub-conscious memory.

Strauss had Faith. It was Shane's worst night-mare come true. Instead of protecting the woman he had grown to love, the woman who had offered him a future, the woman who had offered him her heart, he had put her life in grave danger. There was no question in his mind—Strauss was there because of him, to even the score. This had nothing to do with William Gerrard. It had nothing to do with defense contracts. It was vengeance.

He had expected it to happen sooner or later. It was just a matter of his past catching up with him.

But now Faith was caught up in it as well. She could die, and it would be his fault.

Dammit, he thought, this was why he had avoided involvement. Long ago he had set the rules that governed his life. Those boundaries had made his life a lonely one but that had been the price for doing a very important job, a job he believed in. By breaking those rules he had endangered the one person who had touched his life and left him feeling better for it.

The twinkling lights of Anastasia came into view as the road eased around a bend and down a slope. The tourist town that was home to two thousand permanent residents was nestled in a quiet cove. With its restored Victorian buildings and busy harbor, Anastasia was picture-postcard lovely, but its beauty was lost on Shane. His entire being was focused on one goal—rescuing Faith from the clutches of the most evil man he'd ever known.

Dylan's Bar and Bait Shop was located on the waterfront, in the heart of Anastasia's tidy, thriving marina area. It was a popular establishment, busy most nights, and this night was no exception. Warm amber lights glowed through the building's windows, a welcoming beacon to passersby. Music and laughter floated through the front door as patrons came and went.

Parking his car in the small lot, Shane got out, his narrowed eyes scanning the area as he strode toward the phone booth that stood to the left of the bar's entrance. The scents of fish and fuel and the sea filled his nostrils, but danger was what he sensed stronger than anything. Strauss was nearby; he could feel it.

The phone inside the booth was out of order. Strauss's idea of a joke, Shane supposed, though he found no humor in it. Taped to the glass of the booth was a note with the name *Brutus* and a pier number written in Strauss's neat, almost feminine hand. Using the pen that hung on a frayed string beside the phone book, Shane scrawled BANKS across the top of the note and left the missive taped in place.

He had come alone, as Strauss had instructed, but Banks wouldn't be far behind him. There hadn't been time to argue about strategy. Shane had wanted time to try to deal with Strauss on his own—certain that bringing in more cops would further endanger Faith—so he had given himself a head start.

As he pulled his gun from his shoulder holster,

he wondered just how much trouble he would get into for knocking out his boss. It didn't matter. The odds were against him coming out of this at all, he thought as he started toward a boat called *Brutus* and a confrontation with the man who had sworn to kill him.

The *Brutus* was a powerboat, a midsize luxuriously appointed cabin cruiser fitted out for deep-sea sport fishing. But fishing wasn't on the mind of the man who owned the boat, Faith thought as she sat on the cabin's small built-in sofa, trying her best to keep from shaking visibly.

William had owned a boat very like this one. He hadn't been much interested in fishing either. The *Getaway* had been for impressing people, an ostentatious toy, a place to hold clandestine meetings. But if William Gerrard's uses for his boat had been less than honorable, Adam Strauss's were evil.

"In a way, I'm going to regret killing Shane Callan," Strauss said from his leather-upholstered chair in the corner. In his left hand he held a snifter of cognac. His right hand absently stroked the semiautomatic weapon lying in his lap as if it were a beloved pet cat. A Mozart symphony played in the background.

"A very shrewd, intelligent man, Shane. Well brought up, you know. A Princeton man." He smiled at Faith. "I myself graduated from Brown. A doctorate in behavioral psychology."

Faith guessed she was supposed to be impressed, but she was too damn scared to pull it off. Tugging her cardigan closer around her, she merely stared at her captor with wide, unblinking eyes.

He was a handsome man in a cold, sharp-featured way. Thinning brown hair was combed straight back from his high forehead. The arch of his eyebrows above his narrow dark eyes could only be described as sinister looking. They went well with the cruel, thin line of his wide mouth. He was well dressed and meticulously groomed—right down to his neatly manicured nails. Somehow the fact that he was an educated, fastidious man made him seem even more diabolical in his madness.

In a little corner of her mind Faith noted that this entire scenario was insane. She was just a former business major from Notre Dame, a mother, a woman trying to pursue a quiet dream. How on earth had she ended up on a boat listening to

Mozart while an assassin reminisced about his college days?

"What do you need me for?" She blurted the question out, amazed that she had dredged up the nerve.

Strauss's face lit with amusement. "Why, bait, of course. You should be very familiar with the role by now, I should think."

Faith's skin crawled.

"This has all been a very amusing little game." He took a sip of his cognac, savoring the amber liquid for a moment before continuing. "I managed to acquire a copy of Shane's current case file, thanks to an obliging little secretary at the Justice Department. Pity I had to kill her. At any rate, I thought it rather a clever game to play the part of your tormentor. Rouse all of gallant Shane's protective instincts and so on."

A chill went through her at his calm dismissal of murder, and another shot through her at the thought that she had been used as bait to get to Shane. "You never had anything to do with DataTech or William?"

His lips curled upward as he shook his head.

Faith's eyes strayed to the window. She would

have given anything to feel Shane's arms around her now. At the same time she had to hope she wouldn't see him, because the man in the corner was planning to kill him, and she didn't think she could survive watching that happen.

"Rest assured, Ms. Kincaid. He'll arrive presently."

Setting his brandy aside, Strauss rose from his chair only to settle beside Faith on the cushioned bench. She couldn't suppress a shudder of revulsion as he coiled one arm around her shoulders.

"You see," he said in his lazy voice, "I know Shane very well. His strengths, his weaknesses. His likes and dislikes. For a time we were nearly as close as brothers." He brought his pistol up to caress the silencer against her temple almost lovingly, and his voice turned as cold as the steel of the gun. "Then he betrayed me."

Bile rose in Faith's throat as tears stung her eyes.

"Ah, but alas," Strauss said, his voice heavy with mock regret as he glanced at his gold Rolex, "we have no time to discuss such things." With his arm still around her, he stood and drew Faith along with him. "Our hero should be arriving any minute now. Let's go out on the deck to greet him, shall we?"

Raw fury surged through Shane as he approached the *Brutus,* his gaze focused on Faith and the man who held a gun to her head. Close on fury's heels was fear. He tried to will both emotions away. A clear head was essential in a situation as deadly as this one. Emotions got in the way; they clouded judgment and slowed the thinking process. But it was impossible for Shane to look at Adam Strauss—one arm around Faith's shoulders and a pistol pressed to her temple—and not have a riot of feeling tear loose inside him.

His hand tightened on the grip of his gun as the dark desire to kill snaked through him. He may have been raised in an upper-class home. He may have been educated in one of the finest schools in the country. But primitive instinct easily cut through generations of civilized behavior. Beneath the cop, the scholar, the musician, he was a man, and Faith Kincaid was his woman. If Strauss had hurt her...

Hell, Shane thought, he wanted to kill the man for touching her. Despite all she'd been through, Faith was an innocent. Adam Strauss represented everything evil. The two didn't belong on the same planet, let alone on the same boat.

"Hello, Shane, my old friend," Strauss said in a silky tone that raised Shane's hackles. "How do like my little boat? *Brutus*. I named it after you."

"I'm flattered all to hell," Shane remarked dryly as he crossed the gangplank and stepped aboard.

"I knew you would be. Drop the gun overboard, Irish."

Reluctantly Shane tossed the Smith and Wesson over the side. Strauss smiled at the soft splash that sounded as the gun hit the water.

"Now the little surprise you have tucked into the back of your trousers."

Scowling in the pale glow of the security light, Shane reached behind him and gently eased a small pistol out of his waistband. It joined its companion on the bottom of the Anastasia marina.

"And that little darling you're wearing for a sock garter." Strauss's laughter floated eerily on the damp night air as Shane muttered a stream of curses. "Ah, yes, my friend. I know all your secrets."

"Yeah, you're a regular genius," Shane commented. His expression a blank, stony mask, he turned to Faith. "Are you all right, Ms. Kincaid?"

Faith winced a bit at his cool, businesslike tone. This was not the same man who had held her and loved her fears away. This was Shane the cop, the man who leashed his emotions and instinctively lived in the shadows.

She prayed she would get the chance to see that other Shane again. The one who was so patient with her daughter, who was a tender lover full of sad, sweet music, the one who sometimes looked at her as if he couldn't quite believe she was real. She told herself she would see that man again. All they had to do was get through this nightmare.

Finding her voice with some difficulty, she managed to stutter, "I—I'm f-fine, Agent Callan."

She was terrified, Shane knew, but as she had so many times over the last few weeks, Faith managed to dredge up a little more strength from that well that ran so deep inside her. He watched her swallow down her fear and stick out her little chin. How one woman who seemed so ordinary could have so much heart and courage was a mystery to him, but he loved her for it.

He loved her, and now she could die because of him. The knowledge twisted in his gut like a knife.

"Shane, you cut me to the quick," Strauss said, pouting like a petulant lover. "I've been a perfect gentleman."

"Gentlemen don't kidnap innocent women and hold guns to their heads," Shane pointed out, his voice low and smoky.

Strauss grinned. "Point taken. Let's call it a temporary breach of conduct—rather like your seduction of a federal witness."

The bastard. He knew. He'd been watching them. A muscle jumped in Shane's jaw. His hands clenched at the thought of wrapping them around Strauss's throat. The idea that this piece of scum had any knowledge of the tender, loving relationship that had blossomed between himself and Faith made him sick. But the wisest course would be to ignore the remark as if it meant nothing to him.

"Let her go, Strauss. Your argument is with me."

Strauss's eyes narrowed as if in consideration, but his hold only tightened on Faith's shoulders. "I think not. I know you, Irish. I know your weaknesses, few though they may be. I know your flaws—melancholy, gallantry, and good Irish whiskey. I mean to take advantage of your gallantry. You won't try anything as long as I hold the lovely lassie. Never make an enemy of a friend, my dear Lancelot," he advised. "That enemy will slay you with your own sword."

Shane heaved a sigh and hitched his hands to his lean hips. "You're boring me, Strauss. If you want to kill me, then kill me and be done with it."

"Oh, no." A thread of rage tangled with the madness in his cultured voice. "I won't make it that easy for you, I mean to see you suffer." Jerking his head in the direction of the dock, he ordered, "Cast off. We're going to take a little midnight cruise. Revenge should be a very private thing, I think."

Shane weighed the odds. He couldn't rush Strauss now, Faith would never have a chance. For the moment the deck was stacked in the killer's favor. Obviously Strauss didn't realize it, but sea would take some of his advantage away. So Shane went about the task of setting the *Brutus* free, skills he had learned as a boy surfacing without effort. The Atlantic had been a second home to him when he'd been growing up. He could only hope the Pacific would prove to be as good a friend.

Keeping a firm grip on Faith, Strauss motioned Shane toward the ladder that led to the navigation bridge. "You're driving, Captain Callan." He flashed a wicked grin in the dim yellow light that spilled out of the cabin. "As you can see, I have my hands full."

The muscles in Shane's jaw tightened against the snarl that threatened to curl his lip as he turned and hauled himself up the ladder. He didn't care if he died trying—his life hadn't seemed worth much for a long time—but Adam Strauss was going to pay for putting his hands on Faith.

Faith wasn't sure if the wave of nausea that sloshed through her stomach was seasickness or fear or both. The *Brutus* had been under way for ten or fifteen minutes, bucking through choppy water, when Strauss ordered Shane to cut the engine. Now it bobbed like a cork on the black water, dipping and swaying beneath their feet as the three of them stood in the cockpit behind the cabin.

It was all Faith could do to keep her balance, and she half fell against her captor as the powerboat rocked. Annoyed, Strauss took her hand and pressed it to the gin pole. "Hold on to that, Ms. Kincaid. If you let go, I'll shoot you."

She couldn't keep from looking to Shane for some kind of sign. He was nearly invisible with his dark hair and clothing, like a panther in the night, but she caught his almost imperceptible nod. Her hand closed around the cold metal pole, and her fingertips brushed across a loosely knotted rope. As Strauss's attention swung away from her, she stole a glance.

A heavy block-and-tackle rig hung down from the top of the gin pole and was secured to it with nothing more than a flimsy piece of nylon. Praying wildly Strauss would keep his focus on Shane, Faith began trying to work the knot loose with her fingers. She didn't want to think about what the madman had planned for her, but she knew he meant to kill Shane, and she had to do everything she could to stop him.

"You betrayed me, Shane," Strauss said, raising his voice so his dramatic accusations could be heard above the wind and the sea and the creaking of the boat. He stood with his feet braced slightly apart, his Italian loafers offering footing that was less than sure on a deck slick with mist. The gun he had pressed to Faith's temple was now leveled at Shane. "We were like brothers. You were my friend."

Shane answered him with a curse. "I was doing my job, Strauss. I'd sooner make friends with a cobra."

"I know differently. We're two sides of the same coin, you and I, my darling Shane."

The statement was so close to being accurate, it nearly made Shane sick. He had come so close to that edge, but he had pulled back. He had struggled with the darker side of himself. For a time he had felt he would never escape the shadow of it. Then Faith had let sunlight into his life, and he had felt his soul begin to heal.

Abruptly he pulled back from his thoughts. He had to concentrate, had to find some way to get Strauss's gun away from him. Strauss had said he wanted to play on Shane's weaknesses. Two could play at that game. Adam Strauss had an enormously overinflated ego. It was time to start punching holes.

"I'm sick of your theatrics, Strauss," he said, caustically. He let one foot inch ahead as the deck swayed beneath his sneakers. "Besides being a lousy actor, you're nothing but a two-bit killer with a fake diploma."

Even in the faint light that glowed out of the cabin Shane could see the man's eyes flash with insane outrage. "How dare you! I am a scholar—"

"What's the plan? Kill me, dump me overboard, and make a run for South America with the woman? You'll never make it."

"Don't tell me what I can or can't do, Agent Callan," Strauss fairly spat out the words, his wild-eyed stare riveted to the harsh planes of Shane's face. The boat lurched, and he had to grab hold of the small freezer behind him with his free hand, but he kept his gun and his gaze leveled at Shane. "I mean to kill you both. You'll watch her die little by little, then you'll join her—one drop of blood at a time. And I *will* get away with it. You of all people should know I am capable of anything."

"Too bad for you your abilities don't live up to your ego," Shane said with a sneer, inching another step closer as Strauss slipped again. "You were never anything more than a pathetic little hood with delusions of grandeur. I was never your friend. I loathed you and I pitied you."

Strauss's control snapped. A wild, inhuman cry erupted from his throat as he brought his gun up with both hands on the grip. At that same instant Faith freed the block and tackle and swung it with all her might. The heavy rope and pulley caught Strauss across the chest, knocking his arm aside just as the pistol bucked in his hand.

Shane pounced across the deck with the grace of a striking cougar, his big body slamming Strauss's back into the freezer. Faith bolted for the ladder but froze on the third rung, her attention riveted to the life-and-death struggle in the cockpit.

The two rolled across the small deck of the cockpit, wrestling for control of the handgun Strauss had managed to hang onto. Shane knocked the pistol free by slamming Strauss's arm against the deck. Strauss relinquished the weapon but gained the upper hand in the fight, rolling Shane beneath him and smashing a fist into his face. His second blow met nothing but the solid deck as Shane dodged sideways at the last instant.

As Strauss howled in pain, Shane threw him aside and struggled to his feet. He reached inside the loose sleeve of his sweatshirt and jerked a .25

caliber pistol free of the small holster that was strapped to his forearm, raising it just as Strauss rushed him with a knife.

Faith's scream split the air an instant before the Crack! Crack! of the gunshots.

The expression on Strauss's face as the bullets slammed into his chest was one of utter surprise. Dropping the knife, he stopped in his tracks and looked down at the dark stain spreading across his silk shirt. His legs buckled beneath him.

With the smoking pistol in his hand, Shane stared down at the man who lay sprawled on the deck with his head cocked at an unnatural angle.

"And you thought you knew all of my secrets," he said softly, unable to call up a single ounce of remorse. This man had threatened Faith's life and would certainly have killed her. She would have been only one of many to die by Strauss's hand. Now Adam Strauss would never kill again. "You were wrong, pal. Dead wrong."

Faith eased herself down the ladder, her heart pounding so, she thought it would explode. In her mind's eye she could still see Strauss lunging at Shane, his knife gleaming in the light from the cabin as the blade slashed through the air. Shane could have been killed. But he was still standing, and Faith had never needed anything the way she needed to put her arms around him. On legs that were as wobbly as noodles, she made her way across the short stretch of deck.

"Shane?"

Her voice seemed nothing more than a whisper, but he heard her. He turned and caught her as she threw herself into his arms, burying her face against his chest.

"It's all right," he said in a rough voice as he clutched her to him, relishing the feel of her, soft and alive against him. "You're all right, honey. He can't hurt you now. No one will ever hurt you again."

Faith hugged him with what little strength she had left. "He wanted to kill you. I was so afraid he was going to kill you."

She had been afraid for him. Guilt lashed out inside him. Faith could have lost her life because of him, because of his past, but she had been afraid for him.

"Faith," he said as he stood her away from him.

Whatever else he had meant to say was lost in the next horrible split second.

The faint glint of light on metal caught Faith's eye. As Adam Strauss lifted the gun that had been dropped on the deck during the struggle, she shrieked Shane's name and shoved him aside. The pistol fired once before Strauss fell back, dead. And Faith collapsed to the deck, pain burning through her in one bright, blinding flash before darkness swallowed her up.

"Faith!" Shane screamed, the sound tearing up from the depths of his soul. "Faith!"

He fell to his knees on the pitching deck, turning her over and lifting her limp body in his arms. With shaking fingers he found the pulse in her throat, then he dug a handkerchief out of his hip pocket and pressed it to the wound in her shoulder where blood gushed freely, soaking into the white polo shirt she wore beneath her cardigan.

Tears of anguish streamed down Shane's face. He'd done it. He'd killed the one good person in his life. He'd known from the start not to touch Faith Kincaid. She wasn't from his world, but he'd dragged her into it, and like everything good she would be destroyed by it.

"God, please don't let her die," he mumbled, stroking her damp curls back from her cool, pale cheek. A horrible, empty ache filled his chest as he sucked in a breath. "Please don't let her die."

With gentle, trembling fingers he lifted the delicate heart pendant she wore and pressed a kiss to it. Then he simply held her and sobbed as the spotlight of a coast guard helicopter cut through the gloom and fell on the deck of the *Brutus*.

ELEVEN

"WELL, WHAT'S THE verdict, doctor?"

Pulling the ear tips of her plastic stethoscope down to hang around her neck, Lindy stepped back from her mother's bed. She pursed her lips and planted her chubby hands on her hips. "You're gonna be okay, but I think you prob'ly need lots of ice cream, and you have to take naps when I say so."

The love that shown in Faith's eyes as she smiled at her daughter was absolute and unrestricted. She couldn't begin to describe how it had felt to see Lindy again after the ordeal she'd been through. The thought had crossed her mind more than once when

Strauss had held a gun to her head that she would never see Lindy again, that she would be robbed of the joy of watching her daughter grow up.

On returning home from the hospital the first thing she'd wanted to do was take her baby in her arms and hold her for hours on end, but the sling binding her left arm to her body had prevented her. It would be a week or two before she could give Lindy a proper hug. For the time being she contented herself with running her right hand over her daughter's soft curls.

"I'd say that's very sound medical advice, young lady."

Lindy beamed a smile up at Dr. Moore. The pudgy, bespectacled doctor slipped her a lollipop from the pocket of his tweed jacket and winked at her.

Anastasia's general practitioner of two decades had insisted on seeing Faith settled in at home. He had advised a longer stay in the hospital, but two days had been more than enough for Faith. She had been driven by the need to go home to Keepsake, to surround herself with familiar things and familiar faces—Lindy's chief among them. Having survived a nightmare, Faith had felt compelled to return to the house that had been her dream.

Now the good doctor gave her a very paternal look, his bushy gray eyebrows drawing together over twinkling green eyes. "I want you to get plenty of rest. You're darn lucky that b-u-l-l-e-t didn't do any major damage," he said, spelling the word out so as not to upset Lindy. "As it is, you'll be a few days getting your strength back. Just lie back and let your friends wait on you hand and foot."

"Sounds good to me," Faith murmured obediently, though the idea of having people wait on her had never set very well with her. She had always done for herself. As weak as she felt, though, she figured she could stand having Jayne and Alaina turned loose in her kitchen for a few days, despite their decided lack of domestic skills. The two of them together couldn't boil water.

"I'll check in on you again tomorrow, honey," Dr. Moore said, moving toward the door, black bag in hand. "Call me if you need me."

Faith thanked him, tucking her smile into the corners of her mouth. Dr. Moore had let the women's movement bypass him entirely. He still doled out casual endearments as easily as he did lollipops. Faith knew he didn't mean to be condescending or disrespectful in any way. He was just a nice, fatherly old gentleman who treated all his patients as if they were his own children. It was that kind of friendly warmth that had drawn her to Anastasia in the first place.

Jayne and Alaina stuck their heads in the door as soon as the doctor was through it.

"Feeling up to having visitors?" Alaina asked.

"For a little while," Faith answered, wondering if one of her visitors would be Shane. She hadn't had a minute alone with him since the ordeal. In fact, she thought, with a little shiver of fear, it almost seemed as though he had been avoiding her.

She remembered none of what had happened on the boat after Strauss had shot her. Her memory held fragments of the emergency room—the bright lights, the metallic sounds and antiseptic scents, the sense of urgency as people rushed around. There was no doubt in her mind that Shane had held her—the sense of safety she recalled was unique to being in his arms. But in the hours since he had kept his distance.

"Honey, if you're too tired, we can come back later."

Faith jerked herself out of her musings, looking almost startled to see her friends. Jayne had pulled a chair up beside the bed, and Lindy had immediately scrambled up onto her lap. Alaina, holding herself a little apart as she always did, was leaning against the foot post, a worried frown tugging down her lush mouth.

"No, no, I'm fine," Faith assured them.

Alaina's frown only deepened. "I don't think many people would agree with you, considering what happened."

"It could have been worse." Faith forced a bright smile, needing desperately to lighten the mood. The last thing she wanted was to relive the horror of what had happened. As it was, she knew the black memory would haunt her for the rest of her life. "Like they say in the movies—it's just a flesh wound."

Jayne rolled her eyes, readily taking Faith's cue. "How cliché."

"What's that mean?" Lindy asked, twisting around on Jayne's lap.

"It's what writers in Hollywood get paid for, sweetheart," Jayne replied with a saccharine sweetness that was lost on Lindy. She hugged the little girl and shot Faith a teasing look. "Look on the bright side. When this is all over, I can write your story into a screenplay, Alaina can negotiate the deal, and we'll make a million selling it to TV for a miniseries. Mr. Callan can play himself and become a star."

"Pass," Faith said, shaking her head against the pillows that had been plumped up behind her. "I think I've had about all the notoriety I can stand."

Jayne pouted prettily, tucking a strand of her wild auburn hair behind her ear. "There goes my big break."

"I thought you were all through with Tinsel Town," Alaina remarked dryly.

"I am. It never hurts to have connections, though. What if one of my llamas is destined to become the next Mr. Ed?"

Alaina sniffed. "Sounds like a good argument for owning a library card." She pushed herself away from the bedpost and reached out to tousle Lindy's hair. "Speaking of breaks, I think we'd better give Faith one."

Faith didn't argue the suggestion. The medication Dr. Moore had given her was kicking in, making her feel numb and fuzzy-headed. She managed a smile for her friends, wondering what she would have done without them. "Thanks again for staying with me, you guys. I really appreciate it."

Alaina took hold of Faith's good hand and gave it a squeeze that revealed more of her feelings than she would ever verbalize. "What are friends for if not to trash your house and eat everything in your freezer while you're laid up?"

On her way out Alaina stopped in her tracks and whirled around. "I almost forgot!" she exclaimed, digging a perfectly manicured hand into the deep pocket of the loose-fitting raw silk jacket she wore. "This came for you in today's mail. It's from Bryan. I thought you'd want to open it right away."

It was uncanny how Bryan's little gifts always seemed to turn up when his friends were most in need of a spiritual lift. But Faith had learned not to question it. Bryan didn't seem to think it unusual at all. His only explanation of the phenomenon had been a shrug and a smile.

She examined the small brown package, Christmas-like excitement momentarily overriding the other complex mix of emotions she had been experiencing. The return address on the box was a castle in Ireland. That sounded like a good place for ghost hunting. Faith could only wonder what else Bryan had found there to catch his fancy.

"I can't open it," she said, frowning at her bandaged arm. "I don't have enough hands."

Alaina dispensed with the small box's wrapping and opened the square jeweler's case inside. Faith gave a little gasp. Nestled on a bed of frayed green satin was a man's ring. Hesitantly she lifted it out. It was obviously very old. The gold had mellowed in color with time and wear. Inside the band was an inscription in what Faith presumed to be Gaelic. But the most remarkable feature of the ring was the crest it bore—two intricately intertwined hearts. They were so worn, parts of them were nearly gone, but there was no mistaking what they were.

They were identical to the pendant that seemed suddenly warm against her skin.

The note inside the box read:

Dear Faith,

I found this in Kilkenny and thought you should have it. I think you'll want it when you find the end of your rainbow. I envy the man you give this to. He'll be getting a heart more pure and bright than anything made of gold.

All my love to you and the rest of the Fearsome Foursome,

Bryan

"It's lovely," Alaina said softly. "But why would he send you a man's ring?"

Faith didn't answer. She merely stared at the ring, then closed it in her hand when a knock sounded at her bedroom door.

"Come in."

Shane opened the door but came only halfway through it, as if he were uncertain of the reception he would receive. Faith's gaze met his, and a hundred unspoken questions sang in the air between them.

Alaina glanced from the hard-bitten warrior in the doorway to her friend's tightly closed fist, and shook her head. "Uncanny," she muttered, then cleared her throat delicately. "I'll leave you two alone."

Shane moved into the room but didn't so much as glance at Alaina as she left. All his attention was focused on the woman who lay in the canopied bed. She looked so fragile, so vulnerable. Her pale skin almost matched the prim cotton nightgown she wore. Shadows lingered beneath her shining dark eyes. Shane's heart ached at the thought that she was in that bed because of him.

Faith's heart was pounding as she took in every aspect of Shane's appearance, from the tips of his black shoes to his elegantly cut dark trousers, the dress shirt that spanned his broad shoulders and tapered to his trim waist. His handsome, aristocratic face wore a carefully closed expression, but it didn't quite mask the emotions in his eyes.

What she read in those silvery depths frightened her. Regret. Pain. A tortured anguish that seemed to reach out and clutch at her heart.

She had gotten her wish. Shane had come to see her, but she knew with an ominous sense of foreboding that she didn't want to hear what he had come to say. Digging down deep, she found she had a little scrap of strength left. She wrapped herself around it and prayed it would get her through whatever was to come.

"Hi, stranger," she said, a soft smile curving the delicate bow of her mouth. She gripped that bit of courage a little harder when Shane didn't return her smile with one of his own. Lord, she'd have given anything to see his mouth quirk up on one side in that devastatingly sexy way of his, to have him reach out and caress her cheek with his elegant musician's hand. But he merely stood, a half step back from the side of her bed, out of reach both physically and emotionally.

"How are you feeling?"

"A little woozy." But not woozy enough to dull the pain that came from looking into his eyes.

"I won't stay long. You need to rest," he murmured, stuffing his hands into his pants pockets. Every inch of him ached to hold her, to feel her soft warmth against him one last time, but he wouldn't allow himself the pleasure. If he touched her now, he'd never be able to let her go—and that was exactly what he had to do. "Banks spoke with the prosecuting attorney in Washington. He said he could push back the date of your testimony. He can get a continuance—"

"No," Faith interrupted. "I'll be fine by then. I don't want him to delay anything. The sooner it's over, the better."

The sooner I'm out of your life, Shane added silently. It was astounding how much that thought hurt. All these years he'd gone along on his own, touching no one, needing no one. In a few short weeks this one small woman had so captured him, it would be like tearing his heart out to leave her. And it would be doubly painful because until Faith, he had stopped believing he had a heart to lose.

"I'm leaving for Washington in the morning," he said abruptly, his voice gruffer and more clipped than usual. "Agent Timmons will stay on and escort you back for the trial."

He set his jaw at a stubborn angle and resolutely refused to look at Faith. But then, he didn't need to see her face to know her reaction. He could feel the shock and hurt roll off her in waves that battered his wall of self-control.

"Why?" she asked in a stunned whisper, managing to put all her painful questions into that one word.

He wasn't strong enough to look her in the face and answer. She sounded so hurt, and Lord knew the last thing he wanted was to hurt her more than he already had. He'd known all along she wasn't for him, but he hadn't been strong enough to resist her. His weakness had nearly gotten her killed.

Struggling with the guilt, he prowled around her room and further punished himself by memorizing every detail of it. The wallpaper was a delicate floral print. She had snapshots of Lindy tucked into the frame of the beveled glass mirror above her cherry dresser. There was also a photograph of Faith and her friends in their graduation caps and gowns with Notre Dame's gold dome behind them and a rainbow arching over their heads. The dresser top held a porcelain pitcher and bowl filled with dried flowers.

Everything about the room was delicate and feminine and old-fashioned. The air was sweet with that soft lavender scent he would forever associate with Faith.

Forcing his mind back to the issue, he said, "You knew from the start I couldn't stay. I was nothing less than honest with you, Faith."

She couldn't argue with that. Shane had warned her on more than one occasion that he couldn't make promises, that their relationship would span only the time it took to solve the case. She had known that going in, but it still hurt to hear him reconfirm it. Lord, it hurt. The pain was so sharp, it cut through the haze of medication and eclipsed the throbbing ache in her shoulder.

Stupid, romantic fool, she berated herself. How

many times did she have to learn the same lesson before it would sink in? Shane had come right out and told her she would never possess more of him than his body. Still, she had plunged in headfirst, brimming with Pollyanna optimism, sure that she would be able to change his mind, that she would be the one person able to get behind his defenses and touch the vulnerable, lonely man who lived behind those gray walls of isolation.

Stopping at the foot of the bed, Shane's left hand gripped the carved cherry wood post as if he needed something to steady himself against. "I came to apologize," he said.

For breaking my heart? Faith wondered bleakly. Don't bother. I should be used to it by now.

But when she met his gaze, it was his pain she felt, not her own. It hit her like a blast of cold wind, stunning her, confusing her.

"You could have been killed because of me," he said, his voice thickening with the emotion he had worked so hard to suppress. His hand tightened on the bedpost until his knuckles turned white. "You'll never know how sorry I am that happened."

She would never know the regret he felt not only for her injuries but over what he had lost as well.

The dream of a future with her had been within his grasp until reality had intruded in the form of Adam Strauss. Now Strauss was dead, but the reality was just as alive, just as harsh. He had chosen a lifestyle that didn't allow for dreams.

"Is that why you're leaving?" Faith whispered, her heart immediately taking hope. "Shane, I don't blame you for what happened."

It was clear, though, that he blamed himself. The guilt that etched lines into his handsome face was almost unbearable to see.

"Shane, I love you."

He shook his head, not to deny her statement, but to keep her from elaborating on it. "Faith, don't. It can't work between us. I knew that from the start, and dammit to hell, I should have had sense enough to stay away from you."

"You said you loved me."

"That was a mistake."

Well, he wasn't mincing words, was he? Faith had no idea how she kept from crying out at the pain. It was as sharp as a knife in her chest. Getting shot didn't even compare. She didn't try to keep the tears from rising in her eyes. They flooded her field of vision and brimmed over the barrier of her thick dark lashes. Her throat tightened on a knot of them. That she managed to comment at all was a minor miracle. "I see."

Shane damned himself to yet another eternity in hell as he took in the stricken look on Faith's delicate heart-shaped face. For a man with a degree in literature he had a way with words that no doubt had the great poets rolling in their graves right about now.

Pushing himself away from the foot post, he moved to the chair that had been pulled up beside the bed. Sitting down, he leaned his forearms on his thighs and heaved a sigh. "No, you don't see. I shouldn't have let myself fall in love with you, Faith. It's just not allowed."

She wasn't about to pretend she was sophisticated enough to understand the rules that governed men like Shane Callan. She wasn't. She didn't want to be sophisticated enough to understand a world that left no room for love. "You're not allowed to be human?"

Since he knew he was all too human, Shane chose not to answer her question. "The job I do is important, Faith. It's also very demanding and dangerous. I chose this way of life knowing the limitations, knowing the rules. I broke those rules, and now you're the one paying the penalty."

"But I told you, I don't blame you for what happened."

No, it wasn't in Faith to lay blame, but that was beside the point as far as he was concerned. "Don't you see, honey? Our worlds don't exist on the same plane. What happened with Strauss only proved that."

Finally giving in to the need to touch her, he reached out and gently closed his hand over the fist she clenched so tightly in her lap. "I'm sorry I hurt you. I'm sorry you were hurt because of me. I should never have let it happen."

"You're talking as if I never had any say in the matter," Faith said with a harsh laugh. The man was a rampaging chauvinist, going on about how he should have made this decision or that decision about what *she* did, as if she wasn't capable of making a rational choice herself. "I'm a grown woman, Shane Callan. I make my own decisions."

Raking a hand back through his black hair, Shane looked away from her. "Let it go, Faith. It just won't work. Believe me, I know what I'm talking about."

"But—"

"No, Faith."

The look in his pewter gray eyes stilled the debate on her tongue. He wasn't going to listen to her. The awful truth tolled inside her head like a death knell. Faith squeezed her own eyes shut against the pain, not opening them even when Shane's fingers curved beneath her chin and his mouth brushed across hers. She didn't watch him leave but listened to his footsteps as he rounded the foot of her bed and crossed the hardwood floor. When the door clicked shut behind him, she squeezed her hand tighter around the ring that burned like ice in her fist, and she cried.

She loved Shane Callan with her life, and he was leaving her.

TWELVE

HE WAS DOING the right thing, Shane told himself for the hundredth time as he wandered through the dark, silent house. He had touched Faith's life only briefly, and look what had happened.

She had touched his life, and he would never be the same. Faith had given him a glimpse of joy, a sample of peace and contentment. Damn, but it hurt to have that slip through his hands! It had nearly killed him to walk out of her room that afternoon, knowing she was hurting too. He would rather have taken her in his arms and kissed her tears away.

But he was the reason she was in pain. Her life would be much better without him in it.

He leaned back against the door frame of the ballroom, a cigarette dangling from his lip, his whiskey flask in his hand. Hell, his life would be fine without the complication of a relationship; it had been for years. People didn't try to get close to him. Even when he'd been young, he had always stood a little apart from the crowd. He was a loner. He had always accepted that.

Taking a pull on the flask, he thought about the future. A shudder ran through him that had nothing to do with the fine Irish liquor warming his belly. A few days ago he had sat on the beach with the sun on his face and the wind in his hair, his eye on the sweet serene woman beside him, his ears filled with the sounds of the sea and the laughter of a child. And he had let himself pretend that he could have that life. Now that image had faded, and all he saw once again was a bleak, gray plane. Shadows were his life, not sunshine, not rainbows.

He didn't belong with Faith. Hers was a heart of gold; his was a heart of darkness.

Crossing the polished floor as silently as a cat, he went to the grand piano and flipped on the brass light. Shutting out all conscious thought about both the future and the past, he sat down and spread his long fingers across the cool ivory keys. Closing his eyes, he let his feelings flow directly from his soul to the keyboard.

Faith sat up in her bed, defying her doctor's orders and nature as well. She was exhausted, but she couldn't sleep. She couldn't cry either. She had long since run out of tears. Rubbing her keepsake between her thumb and forefinger, she sat back against the pillows and stared unseeing into the shadows of her bedroom.

Shane would be leaving in the morning. Not because he didn't love her, but because he *did* love her. He loved her and he was leaving her. Did that make any sense at all? Not to a woman, it didn't. It especially didn't make sense to Faith, who had always let her heart rule her head. But it made sense to Shane, and that was what she had to worry about.

She thought of the guilt and pain she had seen in his eyes, and her heart ached for him. Regardless of what she had told him, he blamed himself for what had happened to her, and some deep-seated, antiquated male sense of chivalry dictated that he let her go because of it. Men. Faith shook her head. No wonder the world was such a goofed-up place—men were in charge of it.

The question was. What could she do about Shane's decision to leave? He had made her no promises. She had asked for none. What right did she have to try to hold him there?

Love.

Love gave her the right. If ever she'd known a man who needed love, it was Shane. Wary, cynical, spending his life in the shadows, he needed someone to reach out to him. That wasn't simply Faith's overactive sense of romanticism talking, it was the truth. She knew it with a certainty that radiated a sense of warmth throughout her entire being.

She loved Shane Callan. She hadn't been looking for love when he'd barged into her life with his brooding black scowl and suspicious nature, but she'd found it nevertheless. Perhaps the fact that she hadn't been expecting it made it all the more special. Certainly it made her realize what a gift that love was.

A gift so exceptional deserved to be kept and cherished. She couldn't let Shane walk back into the shadows of a lonely existence without at least trying to make him understand, without at least trying to give him the love he so desperately needed in his life. As hardheaded as he was, he wouldn't be easily convinced to accept it, but she had to try at least.

Moving to Anastasia and buying Keepsake had been a lifelong dream, but deep inside her Faith had nurtured another dream as well—to someday find a man to whom she could give the wealth of love she had stored up inside her, a man who would need her love and cherish her love and love her in return. She knew Shane was that man.

But what if she couldn't change his mind?

The possibility he might reject her sent little jets of fear shooting along under the surface of her skin. After the years of rejection and indifference she had endured with William, she had no great desire to go through it again. And her feelings for William had been nothing compared to what she felt for Shane. If she laid her heart at his feet, and he still walked away...

Gamely she swallowed down the knot of panic

that had lodged in her throat like a stone. No, she wasn't going to consider the possibility of defeat. There was no point in it. If a person let fear stand in the way, she would never attain any dream, and if she'd ever had a dream worth reaching for, it was this one.

Squeezing her little gold heart, Faith lifted it and pressed a kiss to the keepsake for good luck. She eased herself out of bed, amazed at the amount of strength that simple action sapped from her. If getting out of bed left her breathless, following her dream was going to be a heck of a workout, she thought, as she stuffed her good arm into the sleeve of her ivory satin robe and awkwardly pulled the left side up to cover her injured shoulder.

Using the wall for support, she slowly made her way down the hall, music leading her as it had on a fateful night not so long ago. The first time she had heard Shane play had been her first glimpse of the man behind the stony facade, the man she had fallen in love with. The notes that now drifted to her softly through the still, dark house were just as revealing.

The piece he was playing was achingly tender,

soft and sweet. And it filled her with hope. The longing in Shane's music was real and strong. It reached out to her with a poignancy that brought tears to her eyes. This was not the music of a man who had coldly made the decision to walk away from love. This was the music of a man who wanted a dream but felt he couldn't reach for it; who wanted a home but believed he couldn't have one; who ached for love but let duty deny him of it.

Pausing to gather her strength, Faith leaned back against the wall and let the tears roll down her cheeks. They were tears for the beauty of Shane's song, for the pain beneath it. Lord, please let me convince him, she prayed, her teeth digging into her full lower lip as a wave of emotion swept through her.

Ker-thump.

The music stopped abruptly and silence hummed in the air.

Ker-thump.

Faith held her breath as footsteps sounded faintly on the wood floor of the main hall. As they drew nearer, she caught the unmistakable sound of Shane grumbling. She pressed a fist to her mouth to stifle the giggle that threatened—a giggle that became a groan when she heard the soft creak of protest the fourth step of the grand staircase gave every time it was asked to bear weight.

Darn it all. Confronting Shane in her present condition wasn't the most appealing idea she'd ever had, but she was determined, and confront him she would.

"I don't believe in ghosts," Shane muttered under his breath. He crept along the second-floor hall, walking on the balls of his feet so as not to make any sound that might scare off the ker-thumping "spook." "There's no such thing as ghosts."

Isn't there? The question came to him as clearly as if he had spoken it out loud.

No, he answered, only the slight hesitation in his step betraying his uncertainty. He ordered himself to drop the internal dialogue and concentrate on finding whoever or whatever it was clomping around in the middle of the night. It was probably Mr. Fitz. There was a weird old geezer if ever there was one. Ghosts? Bah, humbug.

What about Ellie? that clear, unrelenting inner voice questioned.

Shane bit back a curse as he paused at the end of

the hall, his hand tightening and relaxing, tightening and relaxing on the grip of his gun. *Ellie's dead.*

And her ghost is haunting your soul. Ellie died, and you blamed yourself. You've carried her ghost inside you all these years. Now you're blaming yourself for what happened to Faith. Will you let her ghost haunt you as well?

Faith isn't dead, no thanks to me. She'll be fine as soon as I get out of her life.

Will she?

The image of her crying flashed quickly through his mind. The memory was as bright and sharp as a bolt of lightning, and it cut him to the quick. But he pushed the image away and answered the question with a firm yes.

Will you?

The question hung suspended in his mind. He refused to answer it, and it refused to leave him.

Ker-thump.

He breathed an unconscious sigh of relief as his attention focused once again on the mysterious noise. This time it sounded as if it had come from behind him. He could have sworn it had originated in this end of the hall. Damn, he thought, as he turned and headed back toward the stairs, his concentration wasn't worth spit anymore. He was going to stay up there and find the source of this sound if it took the whole blasted night.

Flattening himself back against the wall, he narrowed his eyes, searching the shadows for any sign of movement. He saw nothing in the pale silver light that fell through the Palladian window. His hearing was sharp enough to pick up the slightest disturbance of the quiet. There were the sounds associated with an old house settling, like the creak of an elderly matriarch's joints as age seeped into them. In the far distance was the indistinct whoosh of the sea surging against the shore. Nearer there was the unmistakable groan of a floorboard.

Shane's even teeth flashed in the dark as a predatory smile tugged at his lips. Ghosts didn't make the floors creak. Every muscle ready to spring to action, he moved along the wall with deceptive laziness. He had his quarry cornered. The sound had come from Captain Dugan's suite, and there was only one way out—the door that was standing ajar before him.

The taste of victory was sweet, Shane reflected, as he slipped his hand around the polished brass knob and eased the door open. He had the bastard who'd been driving him nuts all these nights. And if it did turn out to be Jack Fitz, Shane was going to shake the old coot until his false teeth rattled. If it turned out to be a squirrel, he'd make a fur rug out of the little beast. If it turned out to be—

"Faith!"

How she kept from screaming, Faith didn't know, but the sound seemed to get jammed crosswise in her throat. To have him suddenly behind her shouting her name, had her heart slamming against her breastbone. She wheeled wide-eyed, clutching her nightgown in a white-knuckled fist against her chest.

Shane flipped on the floor lamp that stood in the corner near the window. The scowl that took the place of surprise on his face was blacker than the night. "What the hell are you doing out of bed?"

"Oh," Faith gasped, leaning heavily against the carved post at the foot of the enormous tester bed. She felt as limp and drained as a deflated balloon, but she wasn't about to admit that to Shane. "Don't bother apologizing for scaring me near to death!"

"Scaring you?" Shane said on a growl, his temper only burning hotter as he took in her pallor. She didn't have any business climbing two stairs, let alone two flights of them! "I ought to give you the scare of your life. I ought to take you across my knee! You're not supposed to be out of bed."

"Pardon me for wanting to spare myself the job of filling in bullet holes in my walls," she said dryly, shooting a pointed glance at his brand-new Smith and Wesson. "You can't shoot Captain Dugan, you know. He's been dead for nearly a hundred years already."

He shoved the gun into his shoulder holster, feeling just a tad bit foolish for having pulled it in the first place. "Don't change the subject," he grumbled. "Dr. Moore let you come home on the condition you stay in bed."

"Why should you care?" Faith asked, tilting her little chin up to the unmistakable angle of challenge. "You're leaving in a few hours anyway."

Shane's shoulders sagged. He dragged a hand back through his hair, heaving a weary sigh as he glanced down at the floor. "Dammit, Faith, you know I care."

"I know you're leaving."

"I have to." Why did she have to make this harder than it already was, he wondered as he turned and stared out the window. The only thing he saw as he looked out was the reflection of a lonely man. "My life is back in Washington. What happened to you reminded me of that in a way nothing else could. I don't belong here, Faith."

"Fine," she said, wincing as she forgot herself and tried to shrug. "Then I'm going with you."

Shane wheeled and glared at her. "What?"

"You heard me. I'll go downstairs and pack right now."

"You can't come to Washington with me."

She arched a delicate brow in arrogant question. "No? Just you try and stop me, Shane Callan. It's a free country. I can go to Washington if I want to."

"Faith," he said tightly, advancing on her, pointing a forefinger at her as if it were the barrel of a gun. "I'm warning you—"

"Warn me all you want," she said with a sassy toss of her head. "I'm going."

"What about the inn?"

"I'd rather be with you than the inn. Lord only knows why."

Temper brought a rush of color to Shane's high cheekbones and flared his nostrils. He jammed his hands on his hips just to keep from reaching out and shaking the infuriating little vixen. "Of all the damn, stubborn—"

"You'd better believe it, mister," Faith said, her chin coming up another notch. "I've had it up to here with men manipulating my life. I will not let you walk away just because you think it's best for me. *I* know what's best for me."

"Oh? Was getting kidnapped good for you? Was getting shot good for you?"

"Is running away from love good for you?" Her question was met with a silence so tense it seemed brittle. Shane stared at her as if she had slapped him. She'd hit a nerve. Thank heaven. Oh, please, she prayed as she drew in a slow, deep breath. "That's what you're doing. Running. We have something special between us, Shane. It won't be good for either one of us if you push that away."

Retreating a step, Shane felt all the anger rush out of him. "I'm just trying to save you, Faith. Can't you see that? The life I live doesn't allow for love."

"Then leave it," she said softly, never taking her eyes from his face. "If that's all that's standing between us, leave it. I know your job is important, and I'll share you with it if I have to, but I'll be damned if I'm going to let it take you away from me."

Shane squeezed his eyes shut. Didn't she know

how badly he wanted to take what she offered? Didn't she realize he was doing the right thing by turning away?

Are you? that inner voice questioned.

"Even if I did quit the agency," he said, trying to answer his own doubts as much as he was trying to answer Faith's, "the job would always be a part of me. The things I've done..." His words trailed off on a tight sigh, and he started over. "I've crossed swords with a lot of bad people, honey. I thought I'd left Adam Strauss in the past, but the past will never be entirely behind me. I can't guarantee something like that won't happen again."

"And one of these days while you're busy worrying about it, you're going to step off the curb and get hit by a bus."

Her strange statement pulled Shane away from his melancholy mood. He shot her an annoyed glance, his dark brows riding low over flashing silver eyes. "What the hell is that supposed to mean?"

"It means worrying about something that might never happen is irrational. We can't know what the future will hold. All we can do is grab what we have now and hang on." Taking a big chance that her legs were strong enough to hold her up, she let go of the bedpost and stepped toward him. She locked her earnest gaze on Shane's wary gray eyes. Her heart beat a wild rhythm of hope and fear. "I love you, Shane Callan. You love me. Please don't walk away from that. What we have is far too special to let ghosts and fears steal it away from us."

Oh, Lord, Shane thought as he stared down into those soft dark eyes, I don't think I'm strong enough to walk away from her.

Or was it staying that took more courage? This sweet, good woman was willing to share her life with him. Did he have the guts to put his past behind him and start a fresh new life? He had dreaded the bleakness of his future without Faith, but the idea of loving her and having her love him in return scared the hell out of him. What did he know of love and family? Nothing. Did he even deserve the chance to find out?

With a hand that was trembling slightly, Shane reached out and cupped Faith's rounded cheek. She was so soft. His fingertips tingled where they rubbed against the fine silk of her dark gold curls. The desire to wrap her up and hold her forever was an ache in his chest he was certain would never leave him. She fit in his arms like a puzzle piece that had been missing from his life. He knew he would never feel complete without her.

"I'm a jaded, cynical cop," he said. "I've seen too much of the ugly side of life. I've been a part of that too long. What do I have left to offer you, Faith?"

Her mouth lifted in a smile of infinite feminine wisdom. The love that shone in her eyes was warmer than the sun. "I can live with what you are, with who you've been, but I don't want to live without you, Shane. Offer me your heart, your love."

"You already have them," he whispered.

"Then there's nothing else I'll ever need."

The sense of deliverance, of salvation was so strong, it brought tears to his eyes. The taste of it as he bent his head and settled his mouth softly against Faith's was like nourishment to his starving soul, it was like wine to a man who'd been through a desert. He drank deeply and slowly, savoring every drop.

Faith reached up with her good hand to clutch at Shane's broad shoulder. Relief swept the last of her strength away, and she leaned into him, knowing he would hold her, knowing he would never let her fall. His strong arm banding around her back proved her trust was warranted. Safe in his arms, safe in the knowledge that he was hers, she concentrated on their kiss, on the warm, wild taste of him and the tenderness of his possession.

When he lifted his head, she looked up at him and said, "I have something for you."

Reaching into the pocket of her robe, she pulled out the ring Bryan had sent her and handed it to Shane. He examined it in the soft lamplight, his pulse skipping as he compared the intertwined golden hearts on the face of the ring with the delicate charm that rested against Faith's creamy skin. He read aloud the inscription etched inside the gold band, his voice soft and smoky with emotion. "Two hearts, one destiny."

"You can read Gaelic?" She sounded every bit as incredulous as she looked.

Shane merely blinked at her, as if to say "Can't everyone?" She shook her head and stepped back into the circle of his arms, cuddling against him as best she could, considering her arm was in a sling.

"It figures," she murmured with a soft, sweet smile.

And they held each other for a long time, neither one of them noticing the soft *ker-thump* that sounded in the hall as the bedroom door swung gently shut.

Don't miss the next book in this
romance trilogy by Tami Hoag

Reilly's Return

REILLY WAS GOING to show up sooner or later. It was
fate, destiny, an ominous portent that had appeared
in her morning horoscope. She could feel it in the
bottom of her belly, that deep, hollow sense of im-
pending doom. She could feel it in the weight of the
antique gold bracelet that circled her left wrist with
tingling warmth. That was a sure sign.

It wasn't going to matter a bit that she had left Hollywood and moved up the coast to Anastasia—hun-
dreds of miles away from Tinsel Town in more ways
than just distance. The year of waiting was over, and
he was going to find her.

Jayne Jordan abandoned the wall she'd been
washing, dropping her sponge in the metal bucket
full of soapy water that sat beside her. Tucking her

feet beneath her, she took a deep breath and squeezed her eyes shut as if preparing to dunk her head under water. Heedless of the fact that she was sitting on a scaffolding eight feet above the floor of the stage, she released the air from her lungs and willed herself to relax. Strains of a Mozart serenade floated through her mind as she attempted to banish the sense of dread from her body. Unfortunately, the sweet joyous notes that had poured unblemished from the composer's soul did nothing to erase the image of Pat Reilly from her mind.

She could see him clearly. His image was indelibly etched on her memory. Those breathtaking sky-blue eyes, pale and opalescent, staring out at her from beneath straight dark gold brows; eyes set in a face that was ruggedly masculine. She could feel the intensity of those eyes penetrating her aura, burning through her veneer of restraint and searing her basic feminine core.

It had been that way from their first meeting, and she had cursed both him and herself for it. It had been that way at their last meeting, and it would be that way again, once he found her. And he *would* find her. Pat Reilly was many things, not all of them admirable, but he was nothing if not a man of his word.

Jayne could still feel the mist on her face. She

could see the green of the hills and the gray of her husband's headstone and Reilly as he'd stood before her with the collar of his leather jacket turned up against the wind. She could still taste his kiss, the only kiss they had ever shared, a kiss full of compassion and passion, wanting and guilt, sweetness and hunger. And she could hear his voice—that low, velvety baritone with the Australian lilt that never faded, vowing in a year's time he would return to her. When they both had had a chance to lay Joseph MacGregor's ghost to rest, he would be back.

The year was up.

Jayne sucked in another deep breath as a wave of panic crashed over her. In a valiant effort to fight off the feelings and the memories, she pinched her thumbs and forefingers together to make two circles, held her hands out before her, and began chanting. "Oooommm ... oooommm ... oooommm ..."

The community theater was empty for the moment. Because she hadn't been able to sleep, Jayne had shown up at the crack of dawn to begin cleaning up the building that had stood unused for the past six years. But it wouldn't have mattered if there had been a hundred people present. She would have gone right on chanting had her entire staff of volunteers been gathered around. When a person needed to meditate, a person needed to meditate. It wasn't good for a body to block out its spiritual needs.

"Oooommm...oooommm...oooommm..."

She scrunched her eyebrows together in an expression of absolute concentration and *ooommed* for all she was worth, but it didn't do a darn bit of good. In the theater of her mind the memories played out, undaunted, in all their Technicolor glory. Memories of Reilly proved to be as stubborn as the man himself.

The theater was dark and dank, an unpleasant contrast to the sunny spring morning outside. Pat Reilly ignored the atmosphere. His mind was on more important things than the musty state of the auditorium. He ignored the clutter of junk that had been piled haphazardly backstage, stepping over and around the stuff when necessary, but barely sparing it a glance.

He had followed Jayne Jordan's trail to Anastasia, wondering how long it would take actually to track her down once he got there. But luck had been with him. Driving into the picture postcard coastal village, he had spotted her car—a vintage red convertible MG—slanted drunkenly into a parking spot on a side street with one chrome-spoked wheel on the curb.

If he'd had any doubts about the vehicle being hers—and he hadn't because only Jayne would desecrate the beauty of an antique car with a Save Catalina's Wild Goats bumper sticker—the building the car was parked beside would have settled the question. The marquee was missing several letters, making the building look like an old crone whose teeth were dropping out one by one, but there was enough of the words left so they were understandable. It was the Anastasia Community Theater—a fitting place to find the woman he was looking for.

Now he wound his way through the rubble to the stage proper, following a weird chanting sound. That would be Jayne, he thought, a wry grin tugging at his mouth. The glue beneath the false beard he wore pulled at his skin and he winced. Damn, he probably should have taken five minutes to peel off the disguise. It was his fans he was trying to hide from, not Jayne.

He'd done enough hiding from Jayne and his attraction to her. The time had come for both of them to face facts. Mac was dead and there was nothing standing in their way. It was time to face this damnable attraction that had burned between them from the first time they'd laid eyes on each other, this attraction both of them had denied and cursed and fought against. She had been his best friend's bride, and Lord knew Pat Reilly would have sooner died than betray a mate. But Mac was gone now. A year had passed since they laid him to rest. And there was no reason for the living to go on feeling guilty.

He stopped in the wings, stage left, his booted feet spread slightly. He jammed his big hands at the waist of his well-worn jeans and shook his head as he got his first look at the woman he had come there to find.

Jayne sat atop a rickety-looking scaffolding, her legs twisted into an impossible pretzel design that probably had something to do with yoga or some equally mystical malarkey. She was just as he remembered her: pretty in a way that had nothing to do with cosmetics or fashion. Especially not fashion. Jayne's outfits would have made any other woman look like a refugee from Goodwill. This morning she wore gray thermal underwear bottoms, a purple T-shirt, and a man's gray plaid sport coat that swallowed up her petite frame.

Still, she looked damned appealing to Reilly, proving that hers was an inner beauty that was enhanced by delicate features and eyes like huge pools of obsidian. Her hair was spread around her shoulders in a dark auburn cloud that was nearly black in this light and so wild, Reilly would have bet she couldn't get a comb through it to save her life. But it was soft and silky. He knew that because he'd once buried his hands in it. He'd dreamed of it nearly every night since; every night for a year.

"Oooommm...oooommm...," she chanted, her face a study in concentration as Reilly moved closer.

She had a beautifully sculpted mouth. It was wide and expressive with full, ripe lips. Painted a lush shade of mulberry, those lips curved seductively around the O sound she made and closed softly on the M. Reilly's skin warmed and his mouth went dry as he stared. He could remember exactly the texture and taste of those lips, though he'd sampled them only once, and he had certainly kissed a dozen women since. It was Jayne's taste that lingered on his tongue, sweet and sad and frightened, full of longing and guilt and loneliness. He had craved that taste as if it had been wine. Its memory had haunted him just as the memory of her sweet Kentucky drawl had haunted him.

Memories of Jayne had haunted him more than memories of Mac had, but the thing that had haunted him most was guilt. Now that he saw her, he was all through feeling guilty.